EVERY SECRET LEADS TO ANOTHER

SECRETS *of the* MANOR

Katherine's Story, 1848

BY
ADELE WHITBY

Simon Spotlight
New York   London   Toronto   Sydney   New Delhi

Alfie
Vandermeer

Kate
Vandermeer

Katie
Vandermeer
Goodwin

William
Vandermeer

Eleanor
Wakefield
Vandermeer

Kathy
Vandermeer
Spencer

John
Vandermeer

Sally
Jameson
Vandermeer

Alfred
Vandermeer

Katherine
Chatswood
Vandermeer

Mary
Chatswood

The Chatswood

Family Tree

Beth Etheridge

Gabrielle Trufant

Liz Burns Etheridge

Edwin Etheridge

Beatrice Etheridge Trufant

Claude Trufant

Eliza Tynne Burns

Douglas Burns

Edward Etheridge

Charlotte Gordon Etheridge

Elizabeth Chatswood Tynne

Maxwell Tynne

Cecily Smith Etheridge

George Etheridge

Robert Chatswood

SIMON SPOTLIGHT
An imprint of Simon & Schuster Children's Publishing Division
1230 Avenue of the Americas, New York, New York 10020
This Simon Spotlight paperback edition August 2014
Copyright © 2014 by Simon & Schuster, Inc. Text by Laurie Calkhoven.
Illustrations by Jaime Zollars. All rights reserved, including the right of
reproduction in whole or in part in any form. SIMON SPOTLIGHT and
colophon are registered trademarks of Simon & Schuster, Inc. For information
about special discounts for bulk purchases, please contact Simon & Schuster
Special Sales at 1-866-506-1949 or business@simonandschuster.com.
Designed by Laura Roode. The text of this book was set in Adobe Caslon Pro.
Manufactured in the United States of America 0714 OFF
2 4 6 8 10 9 7 6 5 3 1
ISBN 978-1-4814-1844-7 (hc)
ISBN 978-1-4814-1843-0 (pbk)
ISBN 978-1-4814-1845-4 (eBook)
Library of Congress Catalog Card Number 2013953185

1

I sat back in my deck chair, closed my eyes, and took a deep breath of sea air. No matter how many times I wished it, the paddle steamer *Britannia* would not stop rocking and rolling on the waves of the Atlantic. We could not reach America soon enough to suit my seasick stomach.

Opening my eyes again, I saw my twin sister, Elizabeth, at the deck rail, watching a school of dolphins. They had appeared suddenly after luncheon, leaping and dancing in the waves. They seemed to be performing for the entertainment of the ship's passengers, who surrounded my sister, laughing and calling out to the sea creatures.

I saw one leap above the white foam of the waves and squeal loudly enough for us all to hear. Was it saying hello?

Elizabeth made quick sketches in her drawing pad, catching the essence of the sleek creatures in a few simple lines. No doubt she would include the dolphins in her next painting.

She turned to me, still in my deck chair, my journal unopened in my lap. "Katherine, aren't they the most wonderful things you've ever seen?"

"They're splendid," I said, trying to focus on something other than the lurching in my stomach, but it was no use. The dolphins were indeed splendid, but I would have enjoyed them much more if I had been able to watch them from solid land. My bold sister felt no ill effects from the motion of the ship, but I had been feeling seasick almost from the first moment we stepped aboard the *Britannia*.

It was one of the few differences between us. Elizabeth and I were so nearly identical that when we were born only Mama had been able to tell us apart in an instant. The only obvious physical difference between us was in our hair: Elizabeth's was stick straight while mine fell in waves. That and the fact that Elizabeth was half an inch taller. My twin often joked that she would gladly give me her half inch in height in exchange for my wavy hair.

Right now I'd gladly give her my queasy stomach in exchange for just about anything of hers.

Elizabeth's face fell, seeing my discomfort. "Is it very bad today?" she asked.

I shook my head, not wanting to trouble her. "Not today," I said. "I'm grateful that yesterday's storm has passed, but I am rather tired. I believe I'll lie down for a while before dinner. I'll go and find Essie."

I stood and made my unsteady way toward the passage to our first-class cabin.

As if she had a sixth sense, Essie Bridges, our lady's maid, stepped onto the deck from belowstairs. Like the steadfast friend she was, Essie supported me as I walked shakily across the deck. Minutes later, I was safely ensconced in my bed in the stateroom I shared with Elizabeth.

Essie tucked me in and placed a cool cloth on my forehead. "It won't be long now, Lady Katherine," she said. "I expect you'll feel right as rain the minute your feet touch the dock."

"As long as it isn't moving," I said with a wry smile. "And to think I used to joke about marrying a sea captain."

"Marry a man with two solid feet on the ground, milady," Essie answered. "That's what my da always says."

I couldn't help but smile. Essie and her "da" had recently been united after a lifetime never knowing each other, and she had taken to quoting his wisdom at every opportunity.

Many years ago, Essie's mother, Maggie O'Brien, had been a kitchen maid at our family estate, Chatswood Manor. She kept the fact that she was married a secret from everyone at the manor. Her husband, Sean O'Brien, had sailed to India to earn his fortune. He'd planned to come home or to send for Maggie as soon as he could. Maggie had wanted to train to be a teacher—it was her deepest desire to teach children in her home country of Ireland how to read—and Sean O'Brien wanted to make her dream come true. But by the time he had enough money to send for Maggie, she had disappeared.

Sadly, we learned much later that Essie's mother had died in childbirth. She kept the fact that she was due to have a baby a secret even from her husband and slipped into the village one afternoon on her half day off to find the midwife. The midwife didn't even know the poor young mother's name, only that she was Irish and wished to name her daughter Essie. When the young woman died, a family in the village, named Bridges, agreed to raise the baby as their own, but they honored her mother's wish to call her Essie.

At Chatswood Manor, Maggie O'Brien was simply listed in the staff ledger as a maid who had worked in the kitchens for a few short months before disappearing one afternoon.

Essie herself entered service at Chatswood Manor when she was a teenager. Her warm smile and cheerful nature soon made her our favorite housemaid. When my sister and I were old enough to require a lady's maid, she was our first and only choice. Like Mama, Essie could almost always tell us apart, and she always knew just what to say when we were feeling sad or scared. She wasn't a blood relative, of course, but she was as much family to me and my sister as we were to each other.

When Maggie's husband, Sean O'Brien, came in search of his wife twenty years after she disappeared, Elizabeth couldn't resist the chance to solve a real-life mystery. My adventurous sister talked me into helping her find out what had happened to the mysterious kitchen maid. We had no idea it would lead to our dear Essie being united with her father.

It was a happy, happy day when we made our discovery. Essie, who had helped Elizabeth and me survive the death of our own dear mama, deserved all the happiness in the world. I wondered if she minded our pulling her away on a pleasure trip just a short while after she and her da had found each other.

"Do you miss your father very much, Essie?" I asked.

Essie nodded and gave her customary cheerful smile. "It's the first time we've been apart since we found each other," she said. "But this is a grand adventure, and I wouldn't want to miss a minute of it with my young ladies."

"Mama would have enjoyed it," I said quietly, placing a hand over my necklace.

Mama had died before Elizabeth's and my twelfth birthday, but not before she chose the most special birthday present I could ever imagine. On the morning of our birthday ball this past spring, Papa had

presented me and Elizabeth with two velvet boxes.
Inside, we each found a stunning gold pendant in
the shape of half a heart. Mine was studded in brilliant blue sapphires, as blue is my favorite color. My
sister's was encrusted with red rubies, reflecting her
favorite hue.

When the two halves of the heart are joined
together, a secret compartment reveals itself. Elizabeth
and I wrote a secret message to each other, cut the
letters into confetti, and divided the pieces between
the two necklaces. We promised to pass the necklaces
along to the daughters we would have one day. We
hoped that future generations of girls in our family
would discover the secret message and be inspired to
feel the same love for each other that Elizabeth and
I did.

But it was more than the gemstones and the hidden compartments that made the necklaces so special
to my sister and me. Mama had chosen them for us.
Elizabeth and I wore our necklaces every day, not just
to remind ourselves of our everlasting bond to each
other, but also to keep Mama's love close to our hearts.

"Mama wanted me to have adventures," I said,

thinking about her last letter to me.

"She did, indeed," Essie said, smoothing my hair away from my face.

I closed my eyes, thinking of Mama and of Chatswood Manor and missing them both.

"I miss Mama," I said to Essie. "And home. I long for my own bed—a bed that doesn't roll and lurch."

"We'll be on land again soon, Lady Katherine," Essie said. "I'm sure your papa's American relatives have a lovely room prepared for you, with a bed as comfortable as your own."

I swallowed, hoping for a momentary reprieve from my stomach. "Do you think I don't have the love of adventure that Mama wanted me to have, because I miss home so much?"

Essie shook her head. "I think it means there's lots of love there, milady. It's natural and right to miss it and the people there—I know I do." She smiled. "I even miss crotchety old Mr. Fellows," she said.

I almost giggled, thinking of our dignified butler and how exasperated he could become with Elizabeth and me when we failed to act like proper English ladies, or with Essie when he deemed her too familiar with us. Mr. Fellows had a big heart but often hid it under his dignified demeanor.

"I miss him, too," I said. "I think I'll always miss Chatswood Manor when I'm away from it, even when I'm married. It makes me sad sometimes to think I have to grow up and get married, only to move away."

"That's many years away, milady," Essie said. "Don't borrow trouble from tomorrow. That's what my da says." She placed a new cool cloth on my forehead. "You rest now. I'll be nearby if there's anything you need."

Essie sat in the cabin's comfortable chair, her journal in her lap and a pen in her hand, and watched over me. I breathed in and out, imagining myself at picnic in the gardens at Chatswood Manor, lying on a blanket in the sun the way I sometimes did. The illusion of solid land must have worked. The next thing I knew, my sister was breezing into the cabin. I could tell by the dim light coming through our small porthole that a couple of hours had passed. I had slept.

"Oh, Essie, did you see them?" Elizabeth exclaimed, showing Essie her dolphin sketches. "Weren't they glorious?"

Seeing me in bed, she began to whisper.

"I'm awake," I said, sitting up.

"How are you feeling?" Elizabeth asked.

"Right as rain," I said, repeating Essie's phrase. In truth, my stomach lurched with each dip and roll of the ship, but I was determined not to dampen my sister's joy. I knew she would do the same for me if our situations were reversed.

Elizabeth opened the steamer trunk that we shared. The bottom of the trunk was packed tightly with everything we would need for the coming weeks in America. At the top was what we needed on board the ship—some traveling dresses, formal evening dresses to wear to dinner in the dining room, and whatever we wanted for our amusement. In the trunk's hidden compartment in the lid, we'd stowed away the tools for our favorite pastimes, not because they were secret, but because they were special enough to require safekeeping. For Elizabeth, that was her paints and sketchbook. For me, that was my journal, ink, and pens. Sometimes we combined our efforts. Elizabeth painted scenes to go with my poems and stories, or I wrote stories to go with her sketches and paintings.

10

"I'm glad you're feeling better," Elizabeth said happily. "Cousin Maxwell says we'll arrive in Boston in two days' time—he and Papa took a turn on the deck with the captain this afternoon."

Papa had expressly wished for Cousin Maxwell to join us on our expedition to America so that he would meet our American relations. By law, Papa's title and estate would be inherited by his closest male heir, and that was my thirteen-year-old cousin Maxwell. It was Papa's and Mama's dearest wish that their eldest daughter would marry him one day and become the lady of Chatswood Manor. Elizabeth, being five minutes older than me, was Maxwell's intended bride.

I thought it was romantic and exciting that it had been decreed that she would one day marry Maxwell, especially since he was such a fine and handsome young man. Elizabeth didn't always share that notion. She liked Maxwell well enough, but she often said it would be more much exciting and romantic to wonder about whom her husband might turn out to be, like I could.

"Cousin Maxwell asked about you," my sister said, plopping onto her bed on the other side of the stateroom. "He said he hoped you'd be well enough to join us for dinner."

The warm glow that came over me at the idea of Cousin Maxwell thinking and asking about me almost replaced my seasickness. He and I had become great friends at my birthday ball—in fact, he had mistaken me for Elizabeth and swept me into a waltz for my first dance after the one with Papa. On this trip, we had discovered that we shared many of the same interests. Maxwell had a way of putting me at ease, even when my stomach was flipping over itself with seasickness.

He and Elizabeth did not have the same effortlessness of conversation. I imagine it had something to do with the fact that they would one day be married. It made them shy and stiff with each other.

I didn't want my sister and Essie to see how happy Maxwell's attention made me. Instead I focused on my sister's other news report.

"Two days till we set foot on land," I said. "I can't wait."

Essie shook her head. "Imagine that, milady. Sailing all the way across a vast ocean in just two weeks' time. I can hardly believe it."

"I'm grateful we're on a steamer and not on one of those great big, lumbering ships we saw in Liverpool," I said. "The captain told me it could take them six weeks or more to reach America."

I shuddered, thinking of the long line of people, most of them dressed in what could at best be called rags, shuffling up the gangplank into the side of that vast ship. Next to it, our ship had looked like a toy boat bobbing in a pond.

We had learned just before we left Chatswood Manor that the potato crop in Ireland had failed for the fourth year in a row. Papa said the British government was doing all it could to take care of the people there, but I also knew that Sean O'Brien, and now our Essie, sent every penny they could to relatives in Ireland. Many of the Irish had decided to try their luck in America rather than face starvation at home. Third-class tickets, for accommodations deep in the belly of those slow ships, were the best they could afford. I only hoped they'd survive the long journey.

I shook myself out of my sadness, wishing that all of those travelers would grow rich and fat in North America.

There was another remedy to my sadness at hand. It was time to dress for dinner. Despite my seasickness, dinner had become my favorite part of the day. It was time spent with Papa, my sister, and Maxwell.

*T*hat night over dinner, Papa reminded us of how we were related to the Vandermeers, the American relatives we were on our way to visit.

"Willem Vandermeer is my second cousin," Papa explained. "My grandmother and Willem's mother were sisters. When my grandmother was a young woman, she traveled from the Netherlands to England on a state visit with the Dutch royal family, met my grandfather, and eventually married into the Chatswood family."

"How romantic to give up your home and country to marry a mysterious stranger," Elizabeth said, her eyes sparkling.

"Did they marry for love, Papa?" I asked. I had heard this story before, but this was the first time I had stopped to consider the fact that Papa's grandmother had left her home and family, and also her whole country, when she married. It was brave and sad all at the same time. I wondered if I could ever be courageous enough to do something like that.

Papa considered for a moment. "I'm sure there was an attraction on both sides," he said. "But it was an advantageous marriage for both of them and arranged by their families. Marrying for love is rather a modern notion."

Without even realizing it, I found my eyes had drifted over to Maxwell, and to my surprise, his eyes had found mine, too. I looked down at the untouched dinner on my plate, hoping he wouldn't see the blush creeping into my cheeks.

Papa turned to Maxwell with a twinkle in his eye. "Lady Katherine once told me she planned to marry a pirate," he said. "But I suspect her time at sea has put her off that notion."

Maxwell's eyes flew to me with surprise, and I could feel my cheeks burning even redder.

My twin noticed my discomfort and changed the subject. "And your grandmother's sister married a Vandermeer?" she asked.

Papa nodded. "Piet Vandermeer," he answered. "Willem is their son. I was just about your age when he visited Chatswood Manor with his younger brother, Hans. They were on their way to the United States to start a new life and seek their fortune."

"Have you seen them since?" Maxwell asked.

Papa shook his head. "Hans and his American wife both died a few years ago. He and Willem made a bit of a fortune in the shipping industry and built their manor house in Rhode Island as well as a home in New York City. We've exchanged letters over the years, but Willem has never been back to England. And this is my first visit to America. When Henry Vandermeer wrote to invite us to his wedding, it seemed like the perfect occasion to introduce you and the girls to the American branch of the family."

"Henry Vandermeer is Willem's son?" Maxwell asked.

"Willem never married," Papa answered. "Henry is Hans's son and his uncle Willem's heir. Henry's son, Alfred, is just your age, Maxwell—thirteen."

"We're all looking forward to meeting Alfred," Elizabeth said. "And to seeing an American wedding. Will there be flower girls and bridesmaids like when Lord Bellamy married Mary Smythe two years ago?" She turned to me before Papa could answer. "Remember how much we enjoyed being a part of the wedding? I loved my flower girl dress. It was the prettiest dress I had ever worn until the gowns we had made for our birthday ball."

I laughed at the happy memory. My sister and I had asked Mr. Fellows and the footmen to create a pretend aisle in the great hall and practiced walking down it for days and days. Elizabeth and I were too old now to be flower girls, but we were looking forward to seeing our cousin's wedding. It would take place only a few days after we arrived in America.

Papa patted Elizabeth's hand. "When the big day finally came, Katherine here was so nervous that she dropped her basket of flowers. But the bride didn't seem to mind, did she?"

Elizabeth giggled, but she said nothing. Even Papa sometimes had trouble telling us apart, especially when Essie fixed our hair in an identical fashion.

I giggled along with her. On occasion, confusing people as to which twin was which had worked to our advantage.

Maxwell's eyes, however, were sharper than Papa's. "I've caught you out," he said, eyeing me. *"You're Katherine."*

Papa looked at Elizabeth again and shook his head with a laugh. "I should remember to always look at your necklaces before I speak."

Elizabeth leaned forward and kissed Papa on the cheek. "No matter, Papa."

I was still thinking about the wedding. "Do you think American weddings are very different from English weddings?" I asked.

"I don't know, but I'm sure it will be a lovely event," Papa said. "But Henry Vandermeer and his bride have both been married before and lost their spouses." Papa's face fell for a moment. Life at Chatswood Manor had been lighter and happier since our birthday ball, but we all still were struck with missing Mama sometimes. I think Papa felt her absence most of all.

"I wouldn't expect this wedding to be as grand as if it were the first wedding for both. Nothing like the celebrations we'll have at Chatswood Manor when the two of you are wed," he added.

Papa's comment was directed at Elizabeth and

me, not at Elizabeth and Maxwell, but it was a big reminder that our families intended them to marry. Both of them were careful not to make eye contact, and Maxwell's cheeks turned bright red.

Papa did not notice their discomfort, but I did and changed the subject. "What can you tell us of the bride?" I asked.

"I know almost nothing," Papa said. "Willem only wrote that Mrs. DuMay was a writer with a growing reputation."

"A writer!" I said excitedly, a little louder than I meant to. "I've never met a real writer before."

"You'll have to show her some of your stories," Elizabeth said.

"I'd like to see them, too, Lady Katherine," Maxwell said shyly.

"Oh, I—I don't—," I stammered, not sure if my sudden shyness had to do with showing a real writer my poems and stories or the fact that Maxwell took an interest in my scribbles. I began to cut my food with vigor, hoping that someone would start speaking.

"I wish you knew more about Mrs. DuMay, Papa," I said in an attempt to take the focus off of me. "I want to know as much as possible before we meet her."

"Well, you're in luck, then," Papa replied. "We dine with Captain Braxton tomorrow. No doubt he'll be able to enlighten us about the mysterious Mrs. DuMay. He and Henry Vandermeer are old friends."

Later that evening, after Essie had helped us undress and get ready for bed, Elizabeth and I performed what had become a nightly ritual since our birthday ball.

I took my half of the heart pendant in my hand. "I am Katherine, and I love my sister, Elizabeth," I said.

Elizabeth raised hers. "I am Elizabeth, and I love my sister, Katherine."

We slid the two halves of the heart together to form a single, perfect heart. "Forever," we said at the same time.

Click. Click. Whirrrrrrr.

We heard the gears spinning and the now familiar sound of the hinge, which we could open to reveal the secret panel. We didn't tonight. Ever since we had hidden our note inside, we had left it closed. It was enough to know it was there. If we shook the heart, we could hear the confetti rustling inside.

We kissed each other and then climbed into our beds. I was excited about the prospect of seeing land the morning after next and about meeting our American relations. My mind drifted back to Anna DuMay.

"I'm sure she's very smart and elegant," I said. "I hope she and Cousin Henry are very much in love."

My sister responded with only a contended sigh. Was she thinking of Cousin Maxwell?

"Sometimes I wish my future were as fixed as yours is," I said. "To know whom I am going to marry and where I am going to live. It makes me feel wretched to think of leaving Chatswood Manor someday."

"Sometimes I wish I had your freedom," Elizabeth said, sighing again. "I do long to have an adventure before my life is settled."

I had a thought that made me giggle. "Too bad Cousin Maxwell has learned to tell us apart by our necklaces," I said. "Or we could both have our wishes."

The next night, our last at sea, Elizabeth and I put our questions about Anna DuMay to Captain Braxton. The seas had been calm that day and I felt almost normal. Perhaps it was also the knowledge that when I woke up the next morning, I would be able to see land.

The captain told us as much as he knew about Henry Vandermeer's fiancée. "They are most definitely in love," the captain assured us. Elizabeth and I smiled at each other. "Henry is proud of her writing, too, and says she has every intention of going on with her career after the wedding."

"Have you read her stories?" I asked.

"I have not had that pleasure," he answered. "But I have heard that her reputation is growing. She recently had a great success with a story in a well-known American magazine.

"She's quite independent, I believe," he added. "A supporter of those working to win the right to vote for women."

Papa coughed. "Women voting!" he exclaimed, and I couldn't tell if he disapproved or was merely shocked.

"I think Mama would have welcomed the right to vote," Elizabeth said.

Secretly I agreed. As the captain spoke, I realized that Mrs. DuMay was living exactly the kind of life Mama wished for me in her final letter. Not only was she a published author, but Anna DuMay was an independent woman marrying for love. I wondered if I had it in me to live that kind of life. It's not that I wasn't brave enough, although I wasn't half as bold as my sister. It was more that I loved my life at Chatswood Manor so much that I couldn't imagine a better one. Perhaps Mrs. DuMay would inspire me to cultivate a more adventurous spirit.

"I can't wait to meet her," I said.

"By this time tomorrow," the captain answered, "I believe you will."

3

The next morning, I rushed into a day dress and didn't even give Essie a chance to do my hair before I ran out of the cabin. I had planned to knock on Papa's and Maxwell's doors as I passed, but Maxwell burst into the hall the moment he heard me.

I was the first one upstairs and on the deck. All I saw before me was ocean, endless ocean. My shoulders slumped in disappointment.

Then Maxwell took my arm. I thought perhaps he had confused me with my sister, as so often happened, even with our hair down. But then he said my name.

"Lady Katherine, it's this way." He steered me around to the other side of the ship, laughing at my dismay.

And there it was—land! "Over there!" I shouted, turning to look for my twin. "Land!"

Elizabeth came up behind Maxwell and me. "Boston," she said, clapping her hands.

Realizing that Maxwell's arm was still wrapped around mine, I stepped aside. My arm tingled where his hand had rested.

We were too far away to see much of anything, but there was definitely land peeking out from the horizon. I could barely pull myself away from the deck for breakfast, so anxious was I to reach the shore and to meet our American relatives. I returned as soon as I could and stood watching the city of Boston grow bigger and bigger. Soon I was able to make out buildings and ships and then people moving about on the docks.

A couple of hours later, we reached Boston. Minutes after that, we were stepping onto the gangplank and onto the busy dock.

"How will we recognize the Vandermeers?" I asked Papa. He and Henry Vandermeer had never met, and it had been many, many years since he had seen Willem.

I had barely asked the question when a man dressed in an elegant suit and silk top hat and a boy who looked just like him, only younger and dressed less formally, rushed up to greet us. "Robert Chatswood?" the man asked.

Papa only nodded before the man swept him into an embrace. "Henry Vandermeer," he said. "And my son, Alfred."

Elizabeth and I both curtsied, and Maxwell bowed. It was our English custom. But Henry Vandermeer was American. He hugged Maxwell, Elizabeth, and me in turn. I was afraid Alfred would do the same. I had never hugged a boy before, and I was embarrassed by the whole idea of it. Alfred, thankfully, was more reserved than his father. But instead of bowing like an English boy would, he reached out and gave each of us a hearty handshake. I was astonished and delighted at the same time! Elizabeth must have felt the same way because she was staring at Alfred with a huge, lopsided grin on her face.

"My English cousins!" Alfred exclaimed, kindness and warmth radiating from his robust smile. "It sure is good to finally meet you. Uncle Willem has told me all sorts of tales about the famous Chatswood Manor."

"If it's stories of Chatswood Manor you'd like to

hear," replied my sister, "we have many more."

As Alfred and my sister chattered away, I looked around for the person I most hoped to meet. "Is Mrs. DuMay not with you?" I asked.

"Mrs. DuMay, soon to be Mrs. Vandermeer, has just begun writing a new story and could not be pulled away, I'm afraid," Henry Vandermeer told me.

Before I had time to feel disappointed, we were being rushed toward a handsome coach with six horses. The driver directed the ship's men with our steamer trunks, sweeping Essie and Papa's valet along with them.

The coach was large enough to seat all of us comfortably. Henry Vandermeer lifted Elizabeth and me inside, urging us to sit opposite each other on the coach's two plush benches so that we could each sit beside the window. Alfred and Maxwell followed, sitting in the middle, while Papa and Henry Vandermeer also faced each other. Essie and Papa's valet would sit outside on the high front bench with the driver. I was pleased the day was fine. It would have been an uncomfortable journey for them had it been raining or unbearably hot.

As usual, Essie read my thoughts. She smiled at me through the window just before she climbed up onto the high bench. "I'll have the best view of all," she said, her eyes twinkling.

Minutes later, the horses jolted forward and we were on our way.

Papa and Henry Vandermeer fell into easy conversation. Alfred and Maxwell did the same, talking about the ship and the size of the waves in a storm we had encountered, about sport, and about favorite foods. I was glad to have the opportunity to look out the window and admire the countryside.

The horses clip-clopped their way through the cobbled streets of Boston. It wasn't nearly as big or as old as London, but the city had its simple charms. Soon we picked up the pace and galloped through woods as far as the eye could see. Vandermeer Manor in Bridgeport, Rhode Island, sat on the ocean, but for now I was glad to be rid of the sea. Still, the movement of the coach mimicked that of the boat, and when we stopped at an inn for a light lunch and to change the horses about ten miles into our journey, I was careful not to eat too much.

The small villages we passed through intrigued me. They were nothing like the village near Chatswood, with its High Street and its collection of old, brick buildings. Here the villages were smaller. Many of the houses and inns were built of wood, not stone. We passed small, neat farmhouses and, occasionally, a child ran beside us, waving. One little girl clapped with delight when Elizabeth and I waved back.

Every ten miles or so we stopped to change horses. Henry Vandermeer explained that the Vandermeer horses waited for us at the very last inn we would pass before the final leg of our journey. In all, the trip would take us six or seven hours.

"The road is good," he said. "We haven't had so much rain as to leave us in the mud, or so little as to make us choke on the dust."

It was just growing dark when the coachman entered a long circular drive. Minutes later, we stopped in front of a large stone home with arched windows and a handsome central tower. Vandermeer Manor was lovely. A white marble fountain greeted us with a dancing spray. There were big bow windows on the first floor and pretty little balconies on the second. The grounds were a lush green, and there were many trees and flowers.

I knew the house sat on a cliff overlooking the Atlantic, and I could hear the ocean waves coming in and going out, but the house blocked my view for the moment. That was fine with me.

At Chatswood Manor, Mr. Fellows, the house-keeper, and the rest of the staff would have stood outside to greet guests along with the family. In America, the custom was different. One stately looking man with a full head of white hair waited for us on the stairs lead-ing to the front door. I thought he must be the butler, but like Henry Vandermeer, he swept Papa into a hug.

"Robert, my good man, in my presence again after all these years!" he cried. "You do Henry and Anna a great honor by traveling all this way for their wedding."

After more introductions and even more hugging, Willem Vandermeer insisted that Elizabeth, Maxwell, and I call him Uncle Willem, just like Alfred.

Once we stepped inside the front door, I looked around for Mrs. DuMay. Uncle Willem's good humor dropped a notch when I asked when we might meet her.

"I am sorry she's not here to greet you," Uncle

Willem answered. "The great writer is too busy at her work."

"Uncle, you know that my dear Anna can't wait to meet our English family," Henry Vandermeer said amiably. "But we must leave these creative types to their rituals and routines. Anna says that's where inspiration lies."

Uncle Willem laughed. "Of course, Henry. I wouldn't wish your dear fiancée to be anything other than inspired."

Then he swept us upstairs to our rooms while a group of servants came to help Essie and Papa's valet with our trunks.

Elizabeth and I had connecting rooms, just like we did at Chatswood Manor, only what connected them here was a shared bathroom and not a dressing closet. I was overwhelmed with gratitude to learn that Uncle Willem had checked with Papa about some of our favorite things, including our favorite colors. He had decorated our rooms perfectly to suit us.

My bedroom had blue silk on the walls, with a lovely crisp white coverlet under a white canopy on the bed. Blue silk drapes and chairs matched the walls.

And there was a lovely little dressing table and mirror where I could sit while Essie did my hair. Elizabeth's bedchamber was nearly identical, except that the blue was replaced with red.

The most stunning feature in both of our rooms was the view. The windows on either side of our beds were nearly floor to ceiling, and there was a charming balcony that stretched from one room to the other. It overlooked the manor's grounds and the Atlantic.

Now that I was off the ship and my stomach had mostly settled, I enjoyed watching the waves roll in and out. The sound was soothing, and I knew I would sleep well here, on a bed that didn't roll and lurch, listening to the ocean's rhythms and breathing in the salty air.

Papa's and Maxwell's rooms were just across the hall. They were handsome, too, but rather more masculine. They looked out over the fountain in front of Vandermeer Manor and at the dense woods across the road.

Once we had admired the view, I hoped we would bathe and dress for dinner and then finally meet the bride-to-be, but Uncle Willem and Cousin Henry both thought we might want to rest up after our voyage and our long coach ride. They let us know that dinner would be brought to our rooms.

Essie bustled about, drawing baths, unpacking, and chatting about how pleased she was with her room. "The servants are on the top floor," she said. "And I've got my very own view of the ocean through a small window—imagine that!"

Most of our trunk was unpacked by Uncle Willem's housemaids as soon as we arrived, but we decided to keep some things in there. They were items for which we had no other place to safely store them—like Elizabeth's art supplies, my journal and inks, and two large sunhats that didn't fit in the closets.

Once we were bathed and dressed, Cousin Maxwell and Papa joined Elizabeth and me on our balcony. A housemaid had laid a lovely small table for four, and she and Essie brought up trays of what the cook had described as light supper food. There was tomato soup followed by steamed lobster, corn, and a cold potato salad.

The cook followed up her wonderful dinner with apple pie. She had even cranked out ice cream as a special treat to go along with it. I learned something new about Cousin Maxwell—ice cream was his most favorite dessert in the whole world. We'd have to be sure Mrs. Fields, Chatswood Manor's cook, learned how to churn ice cream before Maxwell's next visit.

Afterward, Papa and Maxwell left us, and Essie helped Elizabeth and me get ready for bed. I was much too overwhelmed with excitement to sleep. So was my sister. Elizabeth brought her sketches and paints into my room and began a dolphin painting while I set to work in my journal, trying to write a poem to go with it, one worthy of showing to Mrs. DuMay.

"Our informal dinner was perfect," I said. "But I did want to meet Mrs. DuMay and find out more about the story she's working on."

"I'm sure we'll meet her at breakfast tomorrow," Elizabeth answered.

I had a sudden thought that made me gasp. "What if she expects us to already know some of her stories?" I asked. "I wish we would have thought to get some, to read on the voyage over."

"Do you want me to ring for a maid?" Elizabeth asked, eyeing the blue silk bellpull next to my bed.

It would ring a bell in the servants' hall, alerting them that the young lady in the blue guest room was in need of attention. "There must be copies in the library here."

I shook my head. "It's too late. I don't want to wake anyone."

"Since Mrs. DuMay's stories have been published only in America, I'm sure she'll understand if we haven't read them yet," Elizabeth said.

"Of course you're right, but I do so much want to make a good impression."

My twin was much bolder than I when it came to meeting new people. She didn't worry about every little thing she said and the impression she made the way I tended to. She came over and gave me hug.

"You *will* make a good impression," Elizabeth told me. "Remember what Mama used to say about meeting new people? Simply ask them about themselves and show an interest. It makes everyone want to know you."

I nodded, feeling the tug at my heart that always came with thoughts of Mama. Her wise words, repeated by my sister, put me at ease about meeting an actual author.

Soon Elizabeth and I were both yawning. We put our pendants together and repeated our nightly chant. Then my sister kissed me on the cheek and went into her room.

I crawled into bed. After so many days at sea, I felt as though I was still rocking and rolling in the waves. I had left the doors to the balcony ajar and could hear the sound of the waves rolling in and out. I had to remind myself that I was on dry land.

Funny how the very thing that made my stomach lurch and roll on the *Britannia* created such a soothing sound. My racing thoughts—wondering what Anna DuMay would be like, whether my American relatives would be enjoyable company, and what Cousin Maxwell was doing—were soon lulled as my breath began to match the ebb and flow of the waves.

I was just dropping off to sleep when I heard a sound that startled me awake again. It was a voice— loud and deep. I couldn't make out the words, but it sounded as if a man was berating someone in a frightful way. I clutched the coverlet to my chest, straining to hear the actual words, but I could not make them out.

Papa was just across the hall and Elizabeth through the connecting doors, but I was too frightened to go to either of them. *What if the man is just outside?* I wondered. *What if he hears me moving about and turns his attention on me?*

Mostly, I wondered, *Who is that? And why is he so angry?*

4

The voice vanished as suddenly as it had appeared. I matched my breathing to the sea again, and soon my heart slowed into the same calm rhythm. The next thing I knew, Essie was opening my curtains, waking me gently just the way she did at home.

"Good morning, Lady Katherine," she sang.

"Good morning, Essie," I answered. I sat up and was greeted by a bright, sunny day under a beautiful blue sky.

Elizabeth must have already been awake. She walked through the bathroom to join us, stretching her arms over her head.

"How did you sleep your first night on dry land, milady?" Essie asked me.

I thought about last night. The troubling voice had gone away so quickly; I realized the whole episode must have been a bad dream. I was overtired and in a strange place. I decided not to mention anything to my sister or to Essie.

"I slept like a dolphin on a gentle wave," I said, thinking about the poem I had begun the night before. "And now that I'm on dry land, my appetite is back. Let's hurry and do something with Lady Elizabeth's hair so that we can go to breakfast."

Elizabeth knew the reason for my desire to hurry. "And meet the famous author," she said with a smile.

"Yes, and meet the famous author!" I answered with a laugh. "I hope I don't get tongue-tied."

Essie gave me a squeeze. "Just remember how much you are loved," she said. "And you've no reason to be afraid of anything."

I chose one of my favorite day dresses in which to meet Anna DuMay—a blue and white striped muslin with puffed sleeves. The neckline showed my blue sapphire pendant to great advantage, and the dress went beautifully with my blue parasol. I imagined the two of us walking together in the garden, talking about literary enterprises, while Elizabeth painted nearby.

Unfortunately, my hopes were thwarted again. At breakfast, Alfred explained that Mrs. DuMay often ate in her rooms when she was in the midst of a new story. I saw Uncle Willem frown upon hearing this explanation, but he said nothing and only urged us to eat our fill.

I began to suspect the author wasn't as interested in meeting us as I was in meeting her. My family had sailed all the way across the Atlantic Ocean. Didn't that call for a trip downstairs to greet us?

I shook off my hurt feelings when Maxwell joined us with a happy smile. Alfred offered to give the three of us a tour of the manor and the grounds as soon as we had finished breakfast.

The customs at Vandermeer Manor continued to surprise me. Breakfast was laid out on the sideboard, and we were expected to serve ourselves. *That makes great sense*, I thought. One could take as much or as little food as one liked, without having to ask, especially since there were so many people staying at Vandermeer Manor, with the wedding only a few days away. Guests and family came and went, sometimes even eating standing up.

The servants, along with the family and guests, were rather more relaxed with us than their English counterparts. No one referred to Elizabeth or me as "Lady." We were introduced as Miss Elizabeth and Miss Katherine, or simply as Elizabeth and Katherine.

Elizabeth seemed to take it all in stride, but I was continually surprised. At one point I looked around to see which one of the maids running past was called Katherine, only to discover that the person, a guest of Henry Vandermeer, was talking to me.

If our butler, Mr. Fellows, were here, he would have corrected everyone with a stern, "Lady Katherine, if you please," but I decided to relax into these American ways. After all, here there were no lords or ladies, I reminded myself. Once I got used to it, it was rather fun.

The house was a bustle of activity with guests arriving, deliveries being made, and servants cleaning every nook and cranny. Alfred, leading us on a tour of the downstairs rooms, explained that the wedding was the late summer's grandest event.

"Even people who don't summer in Bridgeport are

coming to the wedding," he said proudly. "Every home and hotel in the area is filled with guests. Wait until you meet Anna's friends—writers and artists mostly. It's been a treat to get to know them. They're quite different from Father's shipping colleagues."

Elizabeth began to ask Alfred about the painters who might attend when we had to jump back to avoid being knocked over by a man carrying a large, rectangular package wrapped in brown paper. He nodded at Alfred but continued on his way without a word of pardon.

"I say," Maxwell called after him, but the man continued on as if he had not heard.

"That's Uncle Willem's valet," Alfred said. "My uncle must be in a hurry for whatever that is—perhaps a wedding present. I am sorry."

My sister laughed. "I do like these American manners," she said, her eyes flashing. "So much unnecessary bowing and whatnot dispensed with."

Alfred laughed, too. "I am glad you're not shocked by our brash ways," he said.

He led us into the parlor and to a portrait of a woman with a warm smile and friendly blue eyes.

"This is my favorite thing in the whole house," he said. "It is a portrait of my mother. It was painted shortly after she and Father were married."

"She was very beautiful," Elizabeth said. She studied the portrait and then Alfred. "I see a family resemblance, too. You have her eyes."

Alfred nodded, clearly pleased. "She died when I was just a baby. This is the only portrait we have of her. I have no real memories of her, but I have this."

Alfred explained that his parents had been very much in love. So much in love, in fact, that his father had waited nearly thirteen years to remarry.

"I thought he never would, but then he met Anna," he said.

"Are they very much in love, too?" Elizabeth asked.

"I'd say so," Alfred answered. "They were both happy in their independent lives—Anna wasn't wealthy, but she was able to support herself and her son with her writing after her husband died. And my father seemed content with his life. But then they met at a dinner party in New York this spring, and it was love at first sight."

The idea that Papa might remarry flitted across my mind, and I could see my twin had the same thought. I wasn't ready to imagine a new lady of Chatswood. I wanted Papa to be happy again, but if he remarried, I hoped he would wait as long as Henry Vandermeer had.

"Are you looking forward to having a new mother?" Elizabeth asked.

Elizabeth's question made me realize something more. If Papa remarried and had a son with his new wife, then Maxwell wouldn't inherit. Would he and Elizabeth still marry, or would they be free to marry other people? I wondered. My eyes flew to Maxwell, but he calmly waited for Alfred to answer my sister's question. If he worried that Papa might remarry, he hid it well.

Alfred nodded with a smile. "We're all looking forward to having a woman in the house. And, of course, Anna is just wonderful."

"We haven't met her yet," I said quietly. I tried to hide it from Alfred, but my hurt feelings lingered.

"Oh, you mustn't be insulted," Alfred said. "She gets carried away when she begins a new story, but she's been looking forward to meeting you and your sister. I'm sure she'll pull herself away from it this afternoon. I know you'll love her as much as I do when you do meet her."

"Of course we will," Elizabeth said. "I like her already just because she's made you and your father so happy."

"She has," Alfred said with a nod. "Uncle Willem is a little afraid that I'll abandon the family shipping business under her influence and run away to be an artist. I've been so taken with Anna's circle of friends."

"And will you?" Elizabeth asked, her eyes dancing.

Alfred laughed. "I *admire* talent, especially painting," he said. "But I'm afraid I haven't any of my own. It's the family shipping business for me. It's a good thing I love the sea. But who knows what the future will bring. There might be new industries to invest in."

As we continued our tour, Elizabeth asked Alfred about the painter who had done his mother's portrait—apparently the most famous portrait painter in America—and the two of them kept up a steady, easy conversation about the differences between American and English art.

Maxwell and I prowled around the library, finding copies of books by an American author Maxwell was especially interested in—Edgar Allan Poe. His stories sounded dreadfully scary to me, but there was a copy of a magazine with one of Anna DuMay's stories proudly on display. We made a plan to come back to the library as soon as we could for some quiet reading time.

We spent so much time exploring the house that pretty soon it was almost time for lunch. Alfred and Maxwell were engaged for the afternoon—all of the men were going to the races—but our young host promised to show us the grounds and the ocean the next day.

Elizabeth and I went to our rooms to freshen up for lunch. My sister took a few minutes to add some touches to her painting. She was just putting her paints away in the secret compartment in our trunk when there was a knock at my door.

A young woman entered and introduced herself as Tabitha, Anna DuMay's maid, and handed us a note. I read it aloud while Elizabeth looked over my shoulder.

My dearest Lady Katherine and Lady Elizabeth,

Please forgive my failure to welcome you to Vandermeer Manor yesterday. I'm afraid I've been caught up in wedding preparations and in writing a new story.

I do hope you can join me for a private luncheon today in my quarters, where we can properly get to know each other without interruption.

Sincerely,

Anna DuMay

"Please tell Mrs. DuMay we would be ever so delighted to join her," I answered.

Finally, I thought, *I get to meet the author!*

5

At the appointed hour, Elizabeth and I made our way through the manor. As we walked, I marveled at my surroundings. There was so much about Vandermeer Manor that reminded me of home—beautiful paintings lining the walls and plush carpets underfoot—but then so much that was different. After all, Vandermeer Manor was so new, built only over the past fifteen years, whereas Chatswood Manor had been in my family for centuries. Tabitha had said that Mrs. DuMay's quarters were at the very end of the hall in the manor's north wing. Timidly, I knocked on the door, hoping that I wasn't disturbing the writer at her work.

"Come in," called a cheerful voice.

I opened the door and peeked in. A handsome woman stepped across the floor, a newspaper in one hand. "Welcome, girls," she said. "I'm Anna. I am just over the moon that you could join me for luncheon today."

I immediately felt put at ease by Mrs. DuMay's confident manner. "Oh, Mrs. DuMay, I have been so eager to meet you," I blurted out. It was very much unlike me to do so, and I felt a little embarrassed by my outburst.

Mrs. DuMay laughed heartily. "The feeling is mutual," she assured me. "But you simply must call me Anna, my dear."

She gestured toward an area in a corner of the room with four comfortable-looking chairs all facing one another. It was the perfect place for a friendly conversation.

"Now, how shall I tell you apart?" she asked once the three of us were seated. "I see that one of you is taller."

"I'm Elizabeth," my sister said. "I'm taller by half an inch."

"And she's older by five minutes," I added. "And you can also tell which one is which by the pendants we always wear—mine is blue."

"And mine red," Elizabeth added.

Anna admired our necklaces, and I explained that they were a gift from Mama on our last birthday.

"All the dearer to you, then, I'm sure," she said, squeezing my hand. "You must miss her very much."

At that moment I realized that Alfred was right about Anna. She was warm and wonderful, and all of my hurt feelings about not meeting her sooner melted away.

Anna gave us a tour of her quarters. The room we had first entered was a sitting room. Behind it there was a short hall leading to two bedchambers, one for Anna and one for her son, Samuel. Tucked away in a corner of Anna's room was a quiet little alcove with a desk, a chair, and a stack of manuscript pages sitting on a steamer trunk in a style just like ours.

"I can't hear anything back here," she said with a smile. "It's as if the bustle of the house and all of its inhabitants disappear and the only things in the world are my characters and me."

We reentered the sitting room, and Anna rang for luncheon. While we waited, she waved the newspaper she was still carrying.

"Did you girls hear about the Women's Rights Convention that was held in Seneca Falls, New York, earlier this summer?" she asked.

Elizabeth and I hadn't.

"Were you there?" I asked.

"No, but I intend to join these women at the next one, and to work with them to promote the rights of women." She rattled her newspaper again. "The *New York Herald* intends to poke fun at these women by printing their Declaration of Sentiments, but I believe the newspaper has only helped our cause."

Anna leaned in closer to me and Elizabeth, as if she were about to share a secret. "Elizabeth Cady Stanton, a great and brave abolitionist working tirelessly to end the practice of slavery, based this declaration on another great American document, the Declaration of Independence. She declares that women are the equals of men in every way and that we deserve all the same rights and responsibilities—including the right to vote. We must demand a right to have a say in the laws under which we live. It's the very principle our country was founded on."

I was at once breathless and inspired. I had never

given much thought to the power of the vote before. I had always relied on Papa to make the best choices for me and for our family. He had discussed issues with Mama and valued her opinion, but matters of money and laws were ultimately his decision.

I remembered what Elizabeth had said on the ship, and I couldn't help but think that Mama, like Anna, would have been a strong supporter of the Declaration of Sentiments. I found myself wishing that our stay in America might be extended so I could attend the next convention along with Anna. It was just the kind of thing Mama talked about in her letter when she urged me to take advantage of all the new opportunities opening up to women.

I was about to say so when Anna launched into an apology for not seeing us sooner. She had lost track of everything but her story. "When I begin a new piece of fiction, I get so caught up with my characters and the world I create for them that I forget everything else. My fictional characters become as real to me as flesh-and-blood human beings." She laughed a bit. "Thank goodness Henry understands," she said. "Much like the men who signed the Declaration of Sentiments, he encourages me to live a rich, full, and independent life. I believe we'll have a modern sort of marriage. One in which we love and support each other without either one having to let go of our dreams."

My head was spinning with thoughts and ideas about women's rights and marriage and independent lives. Plus, I hoped to learn more about the story Anna was writing now. Was it about these very issues? Would she let me read it in its current state?

I was working up my courage to ask when once again she swept us along to a new topic in her speedy American way. She opened the doors to her armoire and showed us the most exquisite gown I had ever seen. "My wedding gown," she explained.

It was white silk with layers of lace adorning every edge, a fitted bodice and sleeves, and a long, flowing, full skirt. There were ruffles at the neckline, and the edges and hem of the long train were embroidered with flowers in pretty pastel colors.

We had barely begun to admire it when Anna surprised us again.

"Girls, how would you like to be bridesmaids at the wedding?" she asked. "I haven't asked anyone else, and

I'd love to have my new family members participate in what will be one of the happiest days of my life."

I gasped. "Bridesmaids! That would be such an honor," I said. Then I could feel my face fall as I remembered one important detail. "But we're unprepared," I said. "We brought dresses, of course, but nothing special enough for a bridesmaid at your wedding."

"And nothing matching," Elizabeth said. "Katherine and I rarely wear matching dresses like some twins do. Don't bridesmaids' dresses usually match?"

"Oh, I do wish we had thought to pack our gowns from our birthday ball," I said to my sister. "They would have been perfect."

Anna turned to us with a mischievous smile and threw open the other door of her armoire to reveal two dresses made of lilac silk. "Matching bridesmaid dresses!" she announced.

I reached out to touch the fabric. The dresses had high necklines and fitted sleeves, with pretty little ruffles at the collars and wrists. The bodices had elaborate lace dyed lilac, which matched the lace pattern of the bride's gown.

Anna clapped with glee at our astonishment.

"Essie sent me your measurements," she said. "And she told me about how the two of you compromised with purple flowers at your birthday ball."

Elizabeth nodded with a smile. "Our two favorite colors—combined—make purple."

"I thought this lilac would complement my gown beautifully and would be a tribute to my new cousins," Anna said. "I hope we will celebrate many occasions together in the future. The best seamstress in New York made these gowns especially for you."

We barely had time to express our thanks before Tabitha came in with our luncheon on a tray and laid it on the table in the sitting room.

"I've been doing all the talking," Anna said, taking her seat. "Now I want to hear all about you. Tell me about yourselves, your interests."

Anna leaned forward with an interested expression while Elizabeth told her all about our birthday ball and how we had first fooled Cousin Maxwell and then his parents about which one of us was which.

"Maxwell realized his mistake almost immediately, but he danced the first dance with Katherine anyway. His parents, Lord and Lady Tynne, never did catch on.

But our cousin Cecily suspected," Elizabeth said with a laugh. "Our necklaces gave us away."

I recounted the story of Essie finding her father, and the author clapped with happiness. "That would make a great mystery story," she said. "I hope one of you will write it."

"My sister, Katherine, is the writer in the family," Elizabeth said with a smile. "I love to paint and sketch, and she loves to write. We make stories together sometimes. In fact, I'm working on a painting right now of the dolphins we saw in the ocean, and Katherine's writing a poem to go along with it."

"You must let me read it when you're ready," Anna said to me. "And I'd love to see your painting, Elizabeth."

I blushed at her kindness. "I'd love to read the story you're writing now," I said. "Is it about women and independence and the other things we talked about?"

"Indeed it is," she said with a smile. "As a writer, you must know how one's passions take over the imagination."

I was filled with a warm glow to be taken so seriously as a writer.

"Now, tell me about what you like to read. That's the best training for a writer, as I'm sure you know," Anna said. "Who are your favorite authors?"

"We're big fans of Charles Dickens," I told her. "Especially *Oliver Twist*."

"Ah, yes. Mr. Dickens is a great favorite in America as well," Anna said. "He's a wonderful storyteller. People wait on the docks in New York and Boston to get the latest installments of his stories."

"Mama loved Jane Austen, and we do, too," I said, including my sister in my statement. "But I do like rather more excitement in the stories I read."

Elizabeth burst in. "We have something called penny dreadfuls in England. Do you have them here? They're wonderfully thrilling stories about pirates and highwaymen and strange events in mysterious, haunted castles."

Anna laughed. "I have seen them, and they are exciting, indeed."

I didn't want the great writer to think we read only those kinds of tales. "And we read the stories in father's magazines, too," I added.

"Tell me, have you ever read the stories of my friend

Louisa Branson?" she asked. "I believe one or two of her tales have been printed in English publications."

I shook my head.

"I think you'll like her work," Anna said, "especially since you like to solve mysteries." She moved toward her writing room. "She writes stories about a wonderful female detective, a Miss Millhouse, who solves all sorts of thrilling mysteries."

She came back holding two magazines and a sheaf of parchment. "Here are two of her best stories, and a new one she asked me to read before she sends it to her publisher. I'm afraid I've been too busy with the wedding and my own story to send her any comments, but perhaps you can read it and tell me what you think," she said. "I'm sure she'd love to have the opinion of a young writer."

"I—I'd love to read it," I stammered. "But I couldn't presume to give advice to a published author."

"Of course you can," Anna said. "A writer should always invite the opinion of readers. That's how we improve our work."

I was about to ask another question when the author jumped to her feet and swept into her bedchamber. I heard a door open and then some rustling before it closed again. *Did she have a sudden insight into her story? I wondered. Has she left us for her writing chamber?*

A moment later she came back into the sitting room, holding a book and a small box. She handed me the book with a smile, and I saw that it was a lovely hand-made journal with a silk cover and creamy white pages.

"I bought that in Florence, Italy, on a trip last year. I believe you'll find that it's the perfect thing for capturing your stories and poems," she said. "And your thoughts about Louisa Branson's story."

I ran my hand over one of the blank pages. "It's beautiful," I said. "Thank you. I hope my words will be half as beautiful as the pages that hold them."

Anna waved her hand. "Your words are what will make the book beautiful. Don't be afraid to write in it. Make a mistake on the first page and then move on. Never be afraid to make mistakes in your writing. You can always go back and fix things later, but if you expect yourself to be perfect, you'll never get anything down on paper."

I barely had time to register her wise advice before she turned to Elizabeth and handed her the box. "I haven't forgotten you, dear," she said. "I bought these in Florence, too. I didn't know what I wanted them for at the time, but now I do—I was anticipating meeting you."

Elizabeth opened the box to find a lovely set of pastels. "Oh, these are wonderful," she said. "I can't wait to use them."

We left with promises of many happy meetings with Anna DuMay, soon to be Anna Vandermeer, in the coming weeks. I couldn't have been more delighted with our new relation.

At dinner that night, I was pleased to see Anna. Uncle Willem gave her an exaggerated bow when she and Samuel entered the room. "Thank you for joining us," he said.

I thought there might be a touch of sarcasm in his greeting, but Anna only smiled graciously in return. Her son, Samuel, responded with a scowl, but Uncle Willem turned to one of the other guests with his usual friendly smile. He even found a moment to give me, Elizabeth, and Maxwell a wink. We smiled back at the kind older man.

The dining room was crowded with guests from New York and Boston, and I thought Anna and I might not get to talk again, but she made a point of asking to be introduced to Maxwell and introducing us to her fourteen-year-old son, Samuel.

Elizabeth, Samuel, Alfred, Maxwell, and I were all seated together at one end of the table. I thought we would make a jolly party, but Samuel was sullen and distant. Anna had mentioned earlier that day that he was a bit downhearted about moving from New York City to Bridgeport. The Vandermeers had a home in Manhattan, but they spent much of their time at the manor house. I wondered if that was the reason for his displeasure, or if he was melancholy about his mother remarrying. I couldn't imagine anyone having objections to Henry Vandermeer or to his son, but perhaps Samuel saw the marriage as a slight against his father. If Papa remarried, would I be sad?

I shook off those thoughts and turned to Alfred and Maxwell with our happy news. "Elizabeth and I are going to be bridesmaids at the wedding," I said. "Anna told us so at luncheon and surprised us with the most beautiful gowns."

"If there's even going to be a wedding," Samuel muttered under his breath.

"Stop that," Alfred said, his face flushing. "Of course there is."

Samuel shrugged and turned away, saying no more.

I was puzzled by his remark. I could see that my sister was, too. But we both decided it was best not to ask questions.

Still, I couldn't help but turn Samuel's words over and over in my mind. He sounded very sure of himself.

If there's even going to be a wedding. What did Samuel know?

6

That night, I read two of Louisa Branson's published stories before bed. Anna was correct in saying I would enjoy reading them. In fact, I could not put them down once I started them. Miss Millhouse was much like Anna—direct and outspoken but warm and friendly at the same time. She got herself caught up in the most exciting mysteries.

I was in the hands of an expert storyteller, too. In the first story, a mysterious young woman appeared at the home of a New York high society family, claiming to be the daughter who had been lost at sea many years before. I went back and forth many times, believing the young woman was telling the truth and convinced she was an imposter, calling out my opinions to Elizabeth as I read along.

The second story went much faster, mostly because

Elizabeth begged me to stop talking so that she could go to sleep. In this story, a precious family heirloom went missing during a house party in which the detective was present.

In both cases, Miss Millhouse solved the mystery by calm, careful attention and by refusing to settle for easy answers. Even when all the clues seemed to be pointing in one direction and everyone believed the dashing stranger had stolen the jewels, she kept probing until she discovered the truth. It was the secretly destitute cousin from New York all along.

They were brilliant—both the author and her character.

I was too tired to read Louisa Branson's unpublished story, but I couldn't resist reading just the first few pages to see what it was about. It opened with a wedding party, and no doubt something disastrous was about to happen or Miss Millhouse would have no mystery to solve. Perhaps it was best that Anna didn't read it until after her wedding.

I blew out my candle and settled under the covers. I didn't think anything disastrous could occur to ruin Anna and Henry's wedding, but Samuel's strange comment at dinner popped into my mind.

If there's even going to be a wedding.

What could Samuel have meant? I was pondering that when once again I heard voices. An angry rumble reached me, sending chills down my spine. It was followed by knocking and banging. I sat up with the same frightened feeling as the night before, clutching my coverlet to my chest. It was no consolation to me that what I had heard last night hadn't been my imagination.

I strained to hear more and hoped the sounds would go away at the same time. Who was that man talking to and why was he angry?

What would Miss Millhouse do if faced with such a mystery? She would investigate the sounds until she discovered the perfectly practical explanation behind them. I wasn't quite as brave as the fictional detective, so I dashed through the bathroom into Elizabeth's bedroom to find a partner for my search. My sister was sound asleep. I reached out to shake her awake, but standing next to her bed, I couldn't hear anything at all. Where had the sounds gone?

Instead of waking my sister, I crept back into my

own bedroom. I heard the voice and the banging again. I stood next to the wall from which the sounds seemed to come, between my bedroom door and the closet. I heard a lighter voice, probably that of a woman, respond to the angry growl. With shaking hands, I quietly opened my closet door and peered inside. It was empty of everything but my dresses.

"Where is the portrait?" I distinctly heard the voice say. I jumped back. Where was this voice coming from?

I squared my shoulders, took a deep breath, and walked over to the outer door of my room. I opened the door, sure that I would find the source of the commotion in the hall, but no one was there. There was nothing outside my door but an empty hall and quiet nighttime sounds.

Something very curious was going on, but what?

I closed the door, tiptoed back into bed, and slipped under the covers. If we were at Chatswood Manor, I would know where the voices were coming from, but Vandermeer Manor was new to me and I did not know how the sound traveled in the house. And that's when I had the most horrid thought: *Could these voices possibly be otherworldly?*

I was wide awake again but too distracted by my own mystery to return to those of Miss Millhouse. I tried to time my breaths with the ocean waves, as I had done the night before, willing my heart to stop racing. Everyone said that Chatswood Manor was haunted. In a game of hide-and-seek on our eighth birthday, Elizabeth and I thought we saw a ghost in the library. Were angry ghosts the source of the noise I heard? Could Vandermeer Manor be haunted, too? With thoughts of ghosts in my head, it was a long while before I was able to fall asleep.

The next morning at breakfast, Elizabeth and I discovered that Maxwell and Alfred had already eaten and were playing chess in the parlor. As soon as we finished our own breakfast, we sought them out— Alfred had promised us a tour of the grounds today.

On the way, I shared the strange events of the past two nights and wondered aloud if the manor could be haunted.

Elizabeth's eyes danced at the thought. "We will ask Alfred about it," she said.

"I'd rather not," I answered. "He'll think I'm silly.

68

Maybe I did imagine the voices after all."

The boys were sitting under the portrait of Alfred's mother, deep into their game, when we arrived.

"Is Vandermeer Manor haunted?" Elizabeth asked Alfred bluntly.

"Haunted?" Alfred asked.

Elizabeth shared what I had told her about the mysterious voices in the night and the lack of bodies to go along with them.

"I'm sure it's nothing," Alfred said with a laugh. "Vandermeer Manor is only fifteen years old, not nearly old enough to have attracted any ghosts." He looked at Elizabeth out of the corner of his eye, and then his voice took on a deep, ominous tone. "But there is that rumor about the Revolutionary soldiers that are buried on this land. And, of course, nearly every man who helped build the house died a ghastly death." He paused for a moment, looking away. "Did you hear battle cries?"

"Oh, yes, that's it," Elizabeth cried delightedly. "Revolutionary soldiers are lurking about, not knowing that the war is long over!" She grabbed my hand, and I jumped with a scream.

Alfred and Elizabeth burst out laughing.

"I am sorry," Alfred said, seeing my red face. "There are no soldiers buried here. And no ghosts. But I did hear from Uncle Willem that Chatswood is said to have its share of ancient spirits lurking about."

Elizabeth laughed as I took a moment to catch my breath. "It does. Katherine and I thought we saw one once, but that might have been our imaginations running away with us."

"What do you make of the voices I've been hearing in the night?" I asked, having regained my composure. "The first night I thought it might be my imagination, but it's happened twice now."

Alfred shrugged. "The maids and footmen are up around the clock, getting ready for the wedding. I'm sure that's it. No doubt whoever you heard was angry about some overlooked detail."

"There was no one in the hall when I checked," I said.

"But you did say that the voices had started to fade before you opened the door," Maxwell said gently. "Perhaps the people they belonged to had already turned the corner and gone downstairs."

I nodded, but I wasn't convinced. At least Maxwell hadn't participated in Alfred and Elizabeth's ruse. What I had heard didn't sound like staff members getting ready for a wedding. The maids and footmen we had encountered were nothing but happy about the wedding, even with all the hard work that came along with it. That voice was angry about something else.

Alfred was wrong. There was definitely something disturbing afoot. I only hoped it wouldn't get in the way of the wedding.

I had no choice but to put those thoughts out of my head. It was time for our tour of the grounds.

"Will Samuel be joining us?" I heard Elizabeth ask as I ran to fetch our sunhats, as Alfred had suggested it was rather too windy for parasols.

"No, fortunately," Alfred replied. "I presume he'd rather sulk in his room than enjoy the nice day."

I returned quickly, and the four of us were soon strolling on the grounds in the sunshine.

Vandermeer Manor had a lovely, wide green lawn stretching all the way to a white brick wall at the edge of the cliff overlooking the ocean. To one side were formal gardens, and to the other were the stables, carriage house, and a wooden stairway leading down to the sand.

Maxwell and I wanted to tour the gardens, but Elizabeth and Alfred pushed for a walk to the ocean, so we decided to go there first. As we passed the stables, we came upon Uncle Willem and his valet climbing into the coach.

"I've business in Providence," he said with a cheerful wave. "But I'll be back tomorrow."

"Do hurry," Alfred said. "The wedding is the day after tomorrow."

Uncle Willem nodded seriously and motioned to the carriage driver to set off.

It was a long way down to the beach on a weathered wood staircase, nearly as steep as the secret staircase that led to Chatswood Manor's cellar. The waves looked rough today, and the wind whipped about, pulling our skirts this way and that. I kept one hand on the banister and one on my hat. The wind tugged at it, pulling against the bow under my chin. It felt as if a great gust would tear it away at any moment.

"This beach is my favorite place in the whole

world," Alfred said when he reached the bottom step.

My sister and Alfred both ran toward the waves. Elizabeth didn't seem to care that her shoes and the bottom of her skirt were getting sprayed with salt water.

"Isn't it wild and wonderful!" my sister exclaimed over the roar, twirling about in the white foam. "Don't you wish we lived nearer to the ocean?" she asked.

"Not me," I said. "The ocean's beautiful but savage, too. It's so vast. I feel like a tiny speck of a thing beside it."

Maxwell stood back with me. "I'm happy enough in the English countryside," he said amiably. "Give me a smooth, flowing river, or better yet, a trout stream, and I'm perfectly happy."

"That's too tame for me," Alfred said. "The sea is in my blood." He turned to Elizabeth with a grin. "You must come on a sailing trip with Father, Anna, and me. One day we hope to sail down the coast, stopping at ports along the way to visit friends and having adventures. Then we'll continue all the way around South America and up to California before returning."

"It sounds splendid!" Elizabeth took off her bonnet

73

and let the wind whip and tangle her hair. "When I'm grown, I think I'll spend all my time at the ocean," she declared. Then she turned to me with a grin. "Except when I am visiting my dear sister."

"But you'll live at Chatswood Manor," Maxwell blurted. He immediately began to blush, as he always did at the thought of his one-day wedding.

I gazed out to sea, not wanting to witness his and Elizabeth's discomfort.

Then I heard a shriek. Elizabeth's hat had been ripped out of her hands by the wind. Both Alfred and Maxwell ran off after it, laughing and calling out to each other.

Elizabeth came and stood beside me, shouting encouragement at the boys.

We watched it bounce along the sand. Each time the boys came close to it, a wind gust picked up the hat and carried it farther away. It was as if Mother Nature was having a good laugh at the boys' expense. Finally a wave took it and then sent it back again. A laughing Alfred and Maxwell finally made their way back to us, Alfred holding the soggy bonnet.

"I thank you, noble knight," Elizabeth teased. "You

have rescued my bonnet from the evil sea monster."

Alfred laughed and lowered himself into a deep bow. "A knight's duty, milady."

We were laughing still when we made our way back to the house. Elizabeth and I planned to walk the boys back to their unfinished chess game before we went upstairs to ring for Essie—Elizabeth had to change her dress and shoes before luncheon—but we stopped short when we entered the parlor.

Where Alfred's mother's portrait had hung just that morning was now a big, empty space. The painting was gone!

7

Alfred strode across the room to the empty space on the wall. "Where is Mother's portrait? It's been hanging in this same spot every day for my whole life. Why would it be moved now?"

Maxwell, Elizabeth, and I didn't have any answers for Alfred. I knew that if Mama's portrait had suddenly disappeared with no explanation, it would have felt like a kick in my stomach, so I understood why Alfred's face grew redder with every passing moment. "Surely there's a practical explanation," I assured him. "Perhaps it's been moved for cleaning."

Alfred shook his head. "Father would have told me about something like that," he said.

Elizabeth put a calming hand on Alfred's arm. "Why don't you go and find him now?" she suggested. "He'll know why it's been moved."

"Yes, you're right," Alfred said. "There's a practical explanation, and Father will know what it is." He tried to smile at her, but worry creased his forehead.

I remembered what he had said yesterday, about this being the only portrait he had of his mother. We had two beautiful paintings of Mama at Chatswood Manor, and we had had daguerreotypes made in the months before she died. Elizabeth and I had each carried one in a small leather frame on our voyage. They graced our nightstands now. Of course, those kinds of pictures had not yet been invented when Alfred's mother was alive.

"Perhaps Anna did not want the first Mrs. Vandermeer's portrait in such a prominent room," Maxwell said quietly when Alfred was out of earshot. "At least for the wedding."

I shook my head, feeling the need to defend my new friend. "Anna said nothing but nice things about Alfred and his mother at luncheon yesterday. I can't imagine that she would have had the portrait moved. And certainly not without discussing it with Alfred first, at the very least."

Henry Vandermeer returned with his son and was

just as perplexed as we were about the location of the missing portrait. "Don't worry," he told Alfred. "We'll get to the bottom of this."

I thought of Louisa Branson's story about the missing family heirloom. Miss Millhouse began her investigation by questioning the person who knew the most about the comings and goings in the house—the butler. I suggested Henry Vandermeer send for him now.

He summoned Mr. Baxter to the parlor.

"It was here after breakfast when I inspected the room, Mr. Vandermeer," Mr. Baxter said. "I can assure you that I gave no one permission to move the portrait."

Mr. Baxter and Henry then proceeded to question the footmen, one by one, but not one of them had seen the portrait being removed or knew where it might be. Next came the housekeeper and the maids. Even the kitchen staff was examined and any servants of the guests staying at Vandermeer Manor for the wedding. All yielded the same response—no one admitted to seeing anything or to knowing why the portrait had disappeared.

Alfred and Henry Vandermeer's distress grew with each negative response.

"We've questioned everyone on the staff and then some," Mr. Baxter announced. "The only member not here is Mr. Willem's valet, and he departed for Providence this morning."

"How could no one have seen the portrait being taken down and carried away?" Alfred asked his father.

Henry put a hand on his son's shoulder and tried to assure him the portrait would be found. "We'll ask our guests at luncheon," he said. "A portrait that size can't have walked off on its own. Someone must know its whereabouts. Surely there's a simple explanation, especially with all this hustle and bustle in the house."

Elizabeth and I took the opportunity to slip upstairs and find Essie. My sister's dress and hair weren't a sight to be seen at luncheon, and even I trailed sand with every step. I rang for her as soon as we reached my room.

"We must hurry, Essie, and change for luncheon. Have you heard?" Elizabeth asked. "Mrs. Vandermeer's portrait is missing. Poor Alfred."

"It's a terrible thing," Essie said, shaking her head. "But it must be somewhere. I do hope for Mr. Alfred's sake that it will be found soon."

I don't know why I didn't think of it before that moment, but Elizabeth's words made me remember those I had heard the night before. "Portrait!" I said. "I distinctly heard that word last night. It was one of the few words I could make out."

I quickly filled Essie in on what I had heard as I was dropping off to sleep while she helped me into a new day dress. The embellishment on the bodice clashed with my heart pendant, so I slipped it inside, next to my heart.

"I'm not convinced that it was footmen and house-maids getting ready for the wedding like Alfred said," I mused. "What if it had something to do with the missing portrait? Something very sneaky could be underway around here."

Elizabeth thought about it for a moment while she stepped into her own dress. Essie began to comb the tangles out of her hair. "But the portrait was still in the parlor this morning," my sister said. "Don't you think that whoever you heard would have taken the painting last night, when you heard them?"

I nodded, thinking. "There would be a smaller chance of being discovered late at night. Why risk being discovered in a busy house in midmorning?" I remembered Miss Millhouse and how she thought through all possibilities before coming to any conclusions. "Maybe they were thwarted in their efforts last night and did the deed this morning. A busy house, servants and guests running around. That could have been the perfect cover for a thief."

"We've yet another real-life mystery unfolding around us," my sister said. "We must help Alfred get his mother's portrait back."

"You're right," I said. "I can't imagine who would want to take the painting, but we must do everything we can to help."

Essie finished fixing Elizabeth's hair and then nodded at the two of us with satisfaction. "I know firsthand that if anyone can solve a mystery, it's the two of you sweet girls."

Elizabeth rushed to a seat next to Alfred when we entered the dining room. Maxwell took my arm and led me in the same direction. I thought that he, once again, must have confused me with my sister. Our hair was drawn into identical styles with none of my waves to give me away, and we had both changed our dresses.

Maxwell pulled a chair out for me. "Sit here, Lady Katherine," he said.

With a start, I realized that Maxwell had known who I was even though my twin and I were both wearing our pendants under our dresses. Maxwell, like Mama and Essie, was able to tell us apart. It was astonishing that he could do so, when even Papa could not.

I was about to remark on that when Henry Vandermeer made an announcement about the missing portrait and asked all the guests if they had seen anything. "Anything at all," he said, "even if it seemed unimportant in the moment."

I watched all the guests carefully, looking for a telltale smirk or shifty eyes, but everyone seemed genuinely shocked. No one remembered seeing any unusual activity in the parlor and most of the guests had been in and out of the house all morning—visiting other friends in Bridgeport, strolling in the gardens, or walking to the ocean, as we had.

Anna DuMay hadn't come downstairs for lunch.

"She wants to finish her story before the wedding,"

Samuel had said when he joined us. "She's been scribbling away all morning. I don't think she stopped for breakfast, and no doubt her lunch will remain uneaten, too."

I was surprised that no one had told Anna about the missing portrait. Surely this was grounds for disturbing the writer at her work.

Even Samuel seemed distressed about the disappearance of the portrait, but when a search of the house and grounds was organized, I noticed that he slipped away without offering to help.

I thought about Miss Millhouse and the missing jewels. She had led a careful search of the entire house, and I proposed we do the same. Elizabeth, Maxwell, and I explored the house's main level, while Alfred, Papa, and Alfred's father took the upstairs rooms and Mr. Baxter supervised a search of the grounds, including the stables. None of us found the portrait, or even a clue as to what had happened to it.

We gathered in the parlor an hour later. Alfred looked sadly up at the blank space on the wall. The paper that had covered the portrait for all those years was much brighter than the wallpaper surrounding it, allowing us to clearly see the outline of where the portrait should be.

I shared again about the voices I had heard in the night.

"Did you recognize the voice?" Henry Vandermeer asked.

I shook my head. "It was very deep and gravelly," I said. "And angry. I was quite frightened by it."

Papa shook his head. "Deep and gravelly could describe any number of people—servants and guests."

"I will recognize it if I hear it again," I told them. "Of that I'm sure."

Alfred slumped into a chair, staring at the chessboard with unseeing eyes.

His father patted him on the back. "Don't worry, son," he said. "We'll find the portrait, and there will be a perfectly good explanation for its being missing. Perhaps Uncle Willem, when he returns tomorrow, will be able to shed some light on the matter."

"Come," Papa said to Henry Vandermeer. "Let's you and I make another search of the stables. Perhaps we'll turn up something the servants missed."

Alfred rose to go with them, but his father urged

him to stay with us. "Do something fun with the young people," he said. "Try to get your mind off it for a bit."

Alfred nodded, but his heart wasn't in it.

Elizabeth sat across from him and took his hand. "I'm so sorry, Alfred. I can't imagine losing our only portrait of Mama. I wish there was something I could do to help."

"You'll keep your ears open, won't you, Katherine?" he asked me. "Maybe you'll hear something more tonight—something that will lead us to the portrait."

"Of course," I said. "And I'm going to make an effort to talk to each and every one of your guests and your servants until I discover the owner of that voice." I shivered, thinking about how much I didn't want to hear that angry voice again, but it would be worth it to help Alfred.

Alfred's mood lightened for a moment, but then he groaned and slumped back into his chair. "I just realized that you've already heard everyone's voices," he said. "Father spoke to all of the servants and every single one of the guests who was in the house this morning, and you heard them all say that they hadn't seen anything."

Alfred was right, but there was still one person who had been at home at Vandermeer Manor all day who hadn't yet been questioned—Anna.

When I said as much, Maxwell turned to me with a confused expression. "Anna has a deep, angry voice?" he asked.

"No, but she was here all morning, in her writing room. Perhaps she heard something. It's worth asking, don't you think?"

Alfred seemed uncertain.

"This is something that she won't mind being disturbed about," I insisted.

Tabitha answered our knock. Like Alfred, she was uncertain about interrupting Anna, but I assured her this was an important enough matter. In fact, I was a little surprised that neither Henry nor Samuel had thought to tell her what had happened.

"Oh, Alfred, I am sorry," she said, when she heard about the missing painting. "I know how important the portrait is to you."

"Did you see or hear anything that might help us uncover its whereabouts?" I asked.

"I'm afraid not," she answered, shaking her head.

She waved in the direction of an uneaten breakfast tray sitting next to an untouched lunch tray. "I've been shut up in my writing room all day, trying to finish my story. I don't hear a thing when I'm in there."

I could see by the fresh ink stains on her fingers and the manuscript pages strewn about her desk that she had indeed been writing all day.

"What can I do?" she asked Alfred, putting her arm around his shoulders. "How can I help?"

"There's nothing," he said, once again trying—and failing—to smile. "We'll get back to our search. You finish your story."

We made our way downstairs to see if Papa and Alfred's father had discovered anything. They were just back from the stables—empty-handed. We were about to tell them that our inquiries had come up empty too when we all heard a loud thumping noise just over our heads, followed by a cry.

Henry Vandermeer turned on his heel and rushed upstairs, followed by Alfred, Elizabeth, Maxwell, Papa, and me. We found Samuel DuMay in his mother's sitting room, trying to pick up a large, rectangular object hidden under a sheet. His face was red and he was hopping about on one foot. He had obviously dropped whatever he carried on the other.

Anna came out of her writing room just as we reached him.

"What is going on here?" Henry Vandermeer asked. "What's under that sheet?"

Samuel began to stammer an answer, but he saw it was no good. Reluctantly, he bowed his head and ripped the sheet from the object.

It was the portrait from the parlor. And it was horribly vandalized with haphazard streaks of paint.

8

Anna looked at the portrait in her son's hands and gasped. Alfred's mother's pretty face was splattered and smeared with paint.

"I demand to know why you have done this disrespectful thing," Henry Vandermeer said.

"I've done nothing," Samuel answered, his voice low and quiet. "I only—"

"This is the only portrait Alfred has of his mother," Henry Vandermeer interrupted. "Our only remembrance." He choked up for a moment, but he took a deep breath and grabbed the portrait out of Samuel's hands.

"I didn't," Samuel said. "I only found it."

"I only hope the damage you've done can be repaired," Henry snapped, storming off with the painting.

Alfred ran after his father, his face a mask of grief and concern.

Anna DuMay leaned against the wall, her face white.

Samuel turned to her, his eyes pleading. "I didn't do it, Mother. I didn't."

"Please leave me with my son," she said quietly.

Papa, Maxwell, Elizabeth, and I went back to our rooms. I felt as queasy as I had on the ship.

"Those voices I heard the past two nights," I said to my sister. "If only I had mentioned them to Cousin Henry or to his uncle Willem, maybe we could have stopped this."

"You did try to tell Alfred and me," she said miserably. "And we thought there was a logical explanation. Plus, we don't have any idea if those voices even did have anything to do with the portrait being defaced."

But what if they did? I thought. "I should have been braver—like you would have been," I said aloud to my sister. "I should have searched harder to discover the source of the sounds instead of cowering in my bed. I might have prevented this."

Elizabeth gave me a hug. "You didn't cower. You came into my room, looked in the closet and the hall," she said. "Don't blame yourself. Blame Samuel."

"*If* he did it," I said. "He seemed as shocked about the missing portrait as everyone else at luncheon. Maybe what he said was true, and he really did find it already damaged."

"You're much more practical about these things than I am," Elizabeth said with a sigh. "I wanted to fly at him for hurting Alfred, but I suppose we must give some credit to his story."

"I wish we could do something more," I said. "I feel quite helpless." I thought about the dashing stranger in Louisa Branson's story. All clues pointed to him, but Miss Millhouse had kept pushing for the truth and discovered he was quite innocent.

I spotted my new journal on my nightstand and decided to write down everything I could remember, both to make myself feel as if I was doing *something* and because it might be useful later. Elizabeth thought she might paint to try to calm her nerves.

She opened the hidden compartment in our steamer trunk to get our supplies.

Elizabeth stood over her paints, her brow wrinkled in confusion.

"What is it?" I asked.

"My paints," she said. "Someone's been using them."

"Are you certain?" I asked. "Who would know where to find them?"

"I don't know," Elizabeth said. "But see how the tubes are indented and rolled up? They were nearly full the last time I opened this case." Then she gasped. "Oh no! What if someone used *my* paints to damage the portrait of Alfred's mother?"

We were wondering what to do next when Essie knocked on my door.

"Have you heard, Lady Katherine, Lady Elizabeth?" Essie asked. "Terrible news. Henry Vandermeer has canceled the wedding."

"Oh, Essie, no!" I said. I dropped onto my bed, completely shocked. "Canceled the wedding? But why?"

"The damaged portrait was found in Mrs. DuMay's quarters and in her son's hands," Essie said. "I suspect Henry Vandermeer felt he had no choice."

I shook my head. "But Anna had nothing to do with it. I couldn't be more sure of that."

"I can only tell you what I heard downstairs," Essie said sadly. "Mr. Vandermeer instructed the servants to begin taking down all evidence of a wedding. I was there myself when Mr. Vandermeer asked the cook to begin packaging the food to send to the Aid Society in Providence."

"How did he seem, Essie?" I asked. "Was he very angry?"

"No, milady," she said, her eyes filling. "He seemed brokenhearted. He has lost the only portrait of his first wife, and he has now lost his fiancée."

"I feel a little brokenhearted myself," I said.

Essie pulled me into a hug. It felt so good to be embraced by our wonderful Essie.

"Oh, poor Anna!" I said. "She couldn't wait to begin her new life as Mrs. Vandermeer. She'll be brokenhearted, too."

"And poor Alfred," Elizabeth added, putting her arms around the two of us. "He was so happy about the marriage."

"As happy as Samuel was unhappy," I added. "Do you really think he could have done it? Could this be what he had in mind when he made those comments about the wedding at dinner last night?"

"He wasn't pleased about the wedding, that's for

certain," Elizabeth said. "And Alfred mentioned to me that all Samuel talked of was moving back to New York as soon as he could."

"Neither of the voices I heard in the night belonged to Samuel," I said.

"He could have had help," Elizabeth said.

I grimaced. "And to think he might have used your paints to damage the portrait." Then I remembered something more. "His mother has the same style trunk. Samuel would know about the hidden compartment."

"But how would he know that I store my paints in it? Or that I even have paints with me?" Elizabeth mused. "This is a mystery, indeed."

Essie's forehead wrinkled in confusion. "What's this about your paints, Lady Elizabeth?"

Elizabeth explained everything to Essie.

"Have you noticed anyone suspicious in my room?" I asked.

"One of the maids was in here yesterday when I came in straighten up and check to make sure your evening dresses were pressed and ready for dinner," she said. "But I saw nothing amiss. She was merely doing her job."

"Do you know which maid it was?" I asked. "She might have seen something—or someone—with Lady Elizabeth's paints."

Essie shook her head. "Many of the guests brought their own servants with them, and Mr. Vandermeer took on extra help for the wedding. I'm afraid I haven't met everyone. This particular maid was new to me."

"Would you recognize her if you saw her again?" I asked.

"I would, milady," Essie said.

"Could you ask around downstairs? We must find out who did this terrible thing."

"I'll keep my eyes and ears open, Lady Katherine. We'll turn her up." She gave me a big hug. "Don't you worry for minute."

"Maybe Samuel didn't do it," I said, watching Essie leave. "And the wedding can still go on as planned."

"I hope so, but it seems unlikely. He was caught red-handed," Elizabeth answered.

"Maybe that's just what the real thief wants us to think." I scribbled a few notes in my journal and then turned to my sister with a sigh. "Let's go see Anna right after dinner," I suggested. "I know she'll be upset. At the very least, maybe we can bring her some comfort."

Dinner was a rather gloomy affair. Henry and Alfred both took trays in their rooms, as did Anna and Samuel. Many of the guests had gone to hastily arranged dinner parties at some of the other great houses of Bridgeport. Cousin Maxwell did what he could to cheer us up, but I was too worried about our friends to be very good company.

As soon as we could slip away, my sister and I went to knock on Anna's door.

Tabitha answered and showed us into the sitting room. Anna's face was pale and her eyes red. She paced slowly about. I could see that she was downhearted, but there was a strength in her, too, that I couldn't help but admire. She came and took our hands with a sad smile.

"My dears, how good of you to come and see me," she said.

She led us to the small table that we had sat at for luncheon just yesterday.

I told Anna how sorry I was that the wedding had been called off. "I know you didn't have anything to do with defacing the painting," I said.

"Did you know how much Samuel was against the wedding?" Elizabeth asked.

"I know what everyone's been saying. I know what Henry and Alfred believe, but Samuel didn't do it," Anna insisted. "I know it sounds peculiar, but someone is framing us."

I asked a hard question, but I felt I must. "Are you sure? Samuel did seem unhappy about the wedding at dinner the other night."

Anna nodded. "Samuel would have preferred that we stay in New York, but he genuinely likes Henry and Alfred. And he loves me—he wants me to be happy." She took both my hands in hers and looked me in the eyes. "You must believe that."

"If you believe it, I believe it," I said. "We'll do everything we can to find out what really happened and to clear your name."

"Maybe the wedding can still take place as planned," Elizabeth said hopefully.

Anna shook her head. "I don't see how. Even Miss Millhouse couldn't solve this mystery in one day. The wedding was supposed to take place the day after tomorrow."

97

"We'll just have to hurry, then," I said, sounding more optimistic than I felt. "And solve the mystery tomorrow. We'll get to work first thing in the morning."

Anna nodded weakly and said good night.

Elizabeth and I headed back to our rooms, where Essie helped us get ready for bed. She hadn't turned up the maid she had found leaving my room yesterday, but she was able to share all of the servants' gossip. Each and every one of them believed that it was a jealous and angry Samuel who was responsible.

"That's going to make our work that much harder," I said to Elizabeth. "It will be difficult to turn up anyone who had more to gain by canceling the wedding."

Despite my sadness, that night I slept soundly for the first time since I had arrived at Vandermeer Manor. The ocean waves lulled me to sleep, and there were no angry voices to wake me and disrupt my rest.

Elizabeth and I were up early, ready to get to work on solving this mystery. I read Louisa Branson's unpublished story and tried to think about this mystery in the way Miss Millhouse would have. I read over the notes about the voices in my new journal. They were a clue. I was sure of it. Then I tried to make a list of the people who might want to stop the wedding. The problem was, I had only one name on it: Samuel.

If Anna was correct about Samuel being framed, I had to prove it by finding out what really happened to Alfred's mother's portrait. I decided to carry the journal with me to record everything I learned.

At breakfast, I told Maxwell about our plan to solve the mystery and save the wedding and asked him to help. The three of us were whispering about what we could do when Alfred joined us, looking as if he hadn't slept a wink.

"How are you?" Elizabeth asked him.

"Sad," Alfred replied. "At first I was angry, but now I'm just sad. Sad for Anna, sad for my father, and sad for me. I know Anna had nothing to do with this; so does my father."

"But then why cancel the wedding?" I asked.

Alfred pressed his lips together. "Samuel," he snapped. "My father believes that if he is capable of doing such a hurtful thing to his new family, then it's best not to move forward. He's the only one who could be happy about the wedding being canceled."

"That's just it," I said. "We spoke to Anna last night, and she's convinced Samuel didn't do it. She thinks he's being framed."

"I find that hard to believe," Alfred said. "All signs point to him. You heard what he said at dinner the other night. And he's been sullen and unhappy since the day I met him. He made no attempt to be my brother."

"All the same, we're going to look into it," I answered. "We have to try."

Elizabeth leaned forward, putting her hand over Alfred's. "We're not going to give up," she said. "We're going to try to save this wedding for Anna and your father. Maxwell's going to help us. Won't you help us, too?"

"Where do we start?" Alfred said.

"I think we'd better start with talking to Samuel," I answered.

We found Samuel in his room—packing. "Are you here to accuse me, too?" he snapped. "My mother's heart is broken, and everyone's blaming me."

"We just want to find out what happened," I said. "Your mother says you didn't harm the painting. So then help us discover who did."

Samuel dropped into a chair. "My mother's lady's maid, Tabitha, found the portrait in Mother's closet and came to me. We don't know how it got there. Mother was shut up in her writing room all morning and had no idea someone had been in her rooms."

"Why didn't you immediately come to us when you found the portrait?" Alfred demanded.

Samuel flinched in the face of Alfred's anger. "We should have," he answered. "Tabitha was sick with worry that someone would think that my mother had damaged it out of jealousy—although she never had anything but kind words for the first Mrs. Vandermeer. My mother is glad that Henry had such a happy first marriage."

"So you were going to hide the damaged portrait?" I asked.

"I thought if I moved it to another part of the house, no one would suspect us. Then I dropped it," he said with a grimace, "and everyone came running. I know how bad it looked."

"If you didn't splatter paint all over the portrait, then who do you think did?" Elizabeth asked. "You said the other night at dinner that you didn't want the wedding to take place."

"That's not what I said," Samuel said hotly. "I only wondered if it was really going to take place. I'm not at all surprised that someone tried to sabotage it. I'm just sorry that he succeeded."

"He? Who, besides you, would have reason to do such a thing?" Alfred pressed.

Samuel stared at Alfred, a challenge in his eyes. "Your uncle Willem," he said.

"Uncle Willem?" I asked. "He wasn't even here

yesterday. We saw him leave for Providence in the morning."

"And he won't be back until this afternoon. Besides, for what possible reason would he try to sabotage the wedding and hurt us all?" Alfred asked.

"He's been trying to get rid of my mother ever since your father announced their engagement," Samuel said, his mouth twisted in a bitter smile. "Oh, he's gracious and kind when you and your father are in the room, but I've seen the way he looks at my mother when he thinks no one is watching."

Uncle Willem had seemed a little put out that Anna didn't come to meet us when we arrived at Vandermeer Manor, but he hadn't expressed any misgivings about the wedding. I thought Samuel must be mistaken. "How does he look at her?" I asked.

"Like he wishes it were the last time he'd have to share the same room with her," Samuel answered. "He hides it well, but he'll be delighted to learn that the wedding has been canceled."

"This is nonsense," Alfred said. "What evidence do you have?"

"No evidence, but I know what I saw," Samuel said.

"He was alone in the parlor the day after the engagement was announced. I saw him ripping a newspaper to shreds and muttering under his breath before he stalked out. I looked into the wastepaper basket to see what had made him so angry. It was a reprint of Mother's story about a woman seeking the right to vote."

"And that's why you made that comment at dinner?" Maxwell asked.

Samuel nodded. "I think he's been planning to stop the wedding all along, and this is the way he did it."

"Why didn't you ever tell anyone about this?" I asked, making a note of Samuel's story in my journal.

"Who would believe me?" Samuel asked. "He never lets on how he truly feels when he thinks anyone is watching. It's only when he thinks he's alone, or your backs are turned. I've been keeping a close eye on him. I know."

"I don't believe it," Alfred said. "Uncle Willem wouldn't—"

"Believe it or don't believe it," Samuel spat. "Your precious uncle has done the worst he can do now, and I'm glad I don't have to worry about protecting my mother from the likes of him anymore. And to think, I was starting to like it here."

Alfred smarted at that last comment as we left Samuel to finish his packing and went for a walk on the grounds to clear our heads. I believed Samuel was telling the truth when he said he was only trying to protect his mother when he moved the painting, but Alfred and Maxwell had their doubts.

"What we do know for sure is that Uncle Willem wasn't even here," Alfred said.

"So we're completely out of suspects," Elizabeth added.

I looked in my journal, reading my notes about the strange voices and Elizabeth's missing paints. What would Miss Millhouse do?

"Maybe we need to look at things another way," I suggested. "Who knew about the paints in our steamer trunk?" I asked. "And who would have been able to get their hands on them?"

"Maybe Essie has turned up the housemaid she found leaving your bedchamber," Elizabeth said slowly.

"Let's go find her," Maxwell suggested.

We found Essie in our rooms, replacing the fresh

flowers in the vases on our nightstands.

"Did you find that maid you saw in our rooms?" I asked.

Essie shook her head. "But with so much work to do, it's hard to get anyone to stand still for even a moment. Any of the maids could have had a reason to enter your room."

"Keep looking, Essie," I said. "That maid might have the very clue we need."

Fresh out of ideas, I suggested we talk to Anna again. We found her placing her manuscript in her steamer trunk—the one with a secret compartment just like ours.

Elizabeth nudged me and whispered, "Tabitha saw me painting when she came to our rooms the other day. And she'd know about the secret compartment in our trunk since Anna's trunk is the same style. Maybe she's the one who took my paints."

"And Samuel said she's the one who found the defaced portrait. She could be our culprit," I suggested.

After a brief discussion with Anna, we set off in search of her maid. We found her in Samuel's room.

"Master Samuel went for a walk," she said.

"We're here to talk to you," I answered.

Seeing the serious expressions on our faces, she stiffened.

I got right to the point. There was no time to lose. We had to save this wedding. "You knew about the secret compartment in our trunk. Did you take Lady Elizabeth's paints?" I asked.

"And use them to ruin my mother's portrait?" Alfred added.

Tabitha looked away, chewing her bottom lip.

"You did take them, didn't you?" Elizabeth said.

"I did. But it wasn't to damage anything," she said quickly. "I paint, too. I wanted to do something special for Mrs. DuMay for her wedding, so I've been working on a painting." She raised her hands, palms up. "I wanted to finish in time. You weren't in your rooms—I was going to ask your permission—but I had a free hour and you weren't there. I was going to go to town and replace them before you had a chance to notice anything was amiss. I will show you the painting."

Tabitha left the room and came back with a painting of the night sky, glittering with stars and a crescent moon. Under that moon were Anna DuMay and

Henry Vandermeer, gazing into each other's eyes.

"This is quite good," Elizabeth said. "But why don't you have your own paints?"

At that, Tabitha stiffened again. "I used them all up. I didn't bring enough with me from New York. Now, please excuse me. I have to go to the basement for the rest of Mrs. DuMay's trunks," she said. "We're leaving tomorrow morning."

Alfred watched her leave the room. "We're back where we started, and the wedding's still off."

My sister took his hand to comfort him, but I wasn't ready to give up.

"There's something Tabitha's not telling us. Something about her paints. Let's take a look at the closet where she said she found the portrait," I said. "Maybe there's a clue there."

Anna didn't answer our knock. We found an empty room and an empty closet. All of Anna's beautiful dresses had been carefully folded and packed.

"There's nothing here," Alfred said.

"Wait. What's that?" I asked, pointing to a dark line.

There seemed to be a crack in the wall, but when

I looked more closely, I saw that it was the outline of a small door, about half the height of a normal door. I pushed and found myself in a hidden passageway, tall enough to stand in. And there, on the floor, were tubes of paint scattered about.

I heard noise behind me. Anna had come up behind us. "Is there—" she began.

My sister and the boys parted, and she walked between them to stand beside me.

"Oh no!" she said. "Those are Tabitha's paints."

Alfred ran to get Tabitha. When they returned, Anna confronted her with the paints in the closet and asked for an explanation.

Tabitha immediately burst into tears. "I was afraid of this," she said.

"Tabitha, how could you?" Anna asked. "How could you do this to Alfred? To me?"

"I didn't do it," Tabitha said, wiping her tears. "My paints were stolen. I've been so afraid that whoever took them used them to damage the portrait."

"Stolen?" I asked. "Tabitha, why didn't you tell anyone when it happened? Why are we only learning this now?"

"At first I thought I had misplaced them and that they'd turn up. I hardly thought anything of it. But after the portrait was discovered, I worried that my paints had been used to destroy your happiness. And now I see that that is what happened!

"I was afraid to say anything," Tabitha continued, her voice trembling. "I didn't want to be blamed for damaging Alfred's mother's portrait. And I wanted to protect you, Mrs. DuMay. I thought Mr. Vandermeer might think you put me up to it. You must believe me."

"Why should we believe you?" Alfred asked. "You've been keeping things to yourself for days."

"Tabitha's been with me for many years," Anna said. "She's like family to me. I believe her."

I could see that Anna truly did believe her maid. I would have believed Essie in a similar situation, but Alfred was still furious. Elizabeth stood at his side, furious too. I decided to keep probing, exactly like Miss Millhouse would have.

"Do you have any idea who might have stolen your paints?" I asked.

Tabitha shook her head.

"Who knew you had them?"

Tabitha shrugged. "All the servants knew. I worked on my painting downstairs, in my free moments. I don't know how my paints made their way up here. I didn't know anything about this secret hallway."

Alfred was about to question her further when Anna jumped in. "Thank you, Tabitha," she said firmly. "You may go now. I know you have a lot of work to do before tomorrow morning."

Anna turned to the rest of us as soon as Tabitha had left the room. "I believe her," she said. "She was thrilled about my engagement. She looked forward to starting a new life here. Why would she do this terrible thing?" She shook her head. "No. It wasn't Tabitha. It was someone else."

Alfred's arms were crossed, his face a stony mask.

"In any case, the damage is done," Anna said. "The wedding is off." She leaned forward and kissed Alfred on the cheek. "I wanted more than anything to be a member of your family. I'm sorry that's not to be."

She turned to Maxwell, Elizabeth, and me. "I'll say good-bye now. I must make arrangements for a carriage in the morning. I want to leave at first light." She squeezed my hand. "Keep writing, my dear. And send me a story when you're ready. I'd love to read an original Katherine Chatswood tale."

I promised I would and let her know that I would

return Miss Branson's manuscript by the end of the day. Then the four of us watched her leave the room. It was all I could do not to burst into tears the way Tabitha had. Even Alfred, who was so angry a few minutes ago, softened.

"We have no real proof either way. Empty paints don't guarantee guilt or innocence," Maxwell said in a measured tone. "Perhaps we can find more clues."

"And save the wedding," Elizabeth said solemnly.

I was still standing in Anna's empty closet, in front of the secret door. The passageway stretched for quite a distance. "Let's check the passage," I said. "Maybe the culprit left behind more than empty paint pots."

Alfred found us some candles, and we walked down the long, secret hall. More passageways split off to the right and left. When we had gone straight for as long as we could, we came to a set of stairs going down.

"I never even knew this was here," Alfred said. "This hallway must stretch throughout the house."

I heard muffled voices coming from one of the rooms. "The angry voices!" I said suddenly. "They must have been coming from the passageway. Alfred, which of these halls would bring us close to my room?"

He thought about it for a minute. "Let's go back toward Anna's quarters. You rooms will be off of the first hall on the left."

We walked in that direction.

"What now?" Elizabeth asked when we reached the turn.

"Run to my room and tell me if you can hear me," I said.

A minute later, I called out to her. "Elizabeth, can you hear me?" I asked.

Alfred, Maxwell, and I heard a knock on the wall and soon we saw Elizabeth.

"There was another door in your closet," Elizabeth explained. "I simply opened it and followed the sound of your voice. If someone was speaking loudly in the passageway near Anna's closet, it's no wonder it woke you up. I heard you loud and clear."

"See. It wasn't a ghost that I heard," I said to Alfred. "It was the people who damaged your mother's portrait. They were prowling around in here in the middle of the night, plotting, and one of them had a very deep voice."

"And you thought the other might be a woman,

right?" Alfred asked. "It could have been Tabitha and Samuel."

I shook my head. "It was not Samuel's voice I heard. His voice isn't nearly as deep."

"What about the woman's voice?" Maxwell asked.

"It was too muffled," I answered.

"If only you had heard and seen them," Alfred said. "How will we ever find out who did it?"

His spirits had lifted for a moment, but just as suddenly, he was filled with despair again.

"Don't give up yet," Elizabeth said soothingly. "There have to be more clues."

I closed my eyes and tried to think again about what Miss Millhouse would do. "Where's the painting?" I asked. "Maybe there's a clue we missed when we first saw it."

"Father took it to his room for safekeeping," Alfred said. "Until we can consult with an artist who might be able to restore it."

The four of us went to Alfred's father's quarters in the manor's other wing. The painting was propped against the wall in his private library. It was just as shocking this time around to see the paint splattered across the face of Alfred's mother. It covered her smile and her eyes. More paint speckled her hair and her dress. The way it was smeared over her features would make it nearly impossible for an artist to render a similar likeness.

We stood staring at it for a moment and then peered at the back, looking for clues. My sister the painter examined the brushstrokes. We found nothing that could shed any light on the culprit.

"It is rather dark in here," I said finally. I knew that Miss Millhouse liked to see things at the very scene of the crime. "Perhaps if we looked at it in the parlor."

Maxwell took charge in a way I admired. "Alfred, lend me a hand, would you?" he asked, taking one side of the frame.

Alfred took the other, and together the boys carried the portrait into the parlor. They leaned it up against the wall underneath where it had hung. The light from the room's big windows made the portrait look even worse.

Elizabeth examined the carpet underneath. "The way the paint is splattered about on the portrait, you'd think there'd be some on the floor as well. But there isn't."

"So whoever did the damage didn't do it here. They took the portrait somewhere else, into one of the secret passages, perhaps, to add the paint," I said. "There's no closet in this room. I wonder where the entrance is."

We stood back, checking the walls for a telltale crack that would reveal the door to the passageway. I looked all around the painting, and then I noticed something—something important.

There was a sharp outline on the wall where the portrait had hung. A square of wallpaper still looked bright and new. But the paper covering the rest of the walls had faded at least two or three shades.

The portrait and frame leaning against the wall was narrower on both sides than the bright wallpaper above.

"This isn't the original portrait," I said. "This is a copy!"

11

"A copy?" Alfred asked. "What do you mean?"

"Don't you see? This portrait isn't the same size as the outline on the wall," I told him. "You can tell by the wall color. The original painting was the same size as the brighter section of paper."

Maxwell walked up and put the damaged portrait exactly in the middle of the outline. "It's at least four inches narrower on each side," he said. He stood back and looked at the height of the outline. "The length is different, as well."

"Whoever defaced your mother's portrait must have made a copy," I said. "Don't you see? The original might still be intact."

"Oh, Alfred. How wonderful!" Elizabeth exclaimed. "I'm so happy for you."

"I must tell Father!" Alfred said, running out of the room. "Maybe we can save the wedding after all."

We ran after him. Henry Vandermeer and Papa were in the library with Uncle Willem, who had just returned from Providence.

Anna had entered the room just before we did.

"I'm leaving very early in the morning," we heard her saying, emotion in her voice. "I came to say good-bye, Henry. I'm sorry things turned out the way they did. Please accept my sincere wishes for a long and happy life." She turned to leave, hesitated, and then looked him in the eye again. "I hope you find love again. I will love you for as long as I live."

Henry's face was strained and sad. Uncle Willem's eyes, however, were filled with anger. He was just about to say something when Alfred stepped up and shared what we had discovered.

"So whoever did it," Alfred finished, "may not have harmed the original. Mother's portrait may still be intact and hidden somewhere."

"None of this makes any sense," Henry Vandermeer said. "Where is the original? And why would Samuel deface a *copy* of the portrait?"

Anna stiffened at the mention of her son's name. "I am happy for you, Alfred," she said quietly. "I hope you find the portrait in its original condition." She nodded at the rest of us and turned to leave the room.

Alfred put a hand on her arm. "Wait, please." Then he turned to his father. "That's just it," Alfred said. "We don't think Samuel had anything to do with it. We think he was framed."

Henry Vandermeer looked from Alfred to Anna and back again. "Who would have done such a thing?" he asked.

I spoke up. "Someone who didn't want your marriage to take place." I kept my eyes on Uncle Willem, remembering what Samuel had said. I still found it hard to believe that Uncle Willem had been behind the plot to sabotage the wedding. I saw how angry he was on Henry and Alfred's behalf. He loved his nephew and his great-nephew. That was clear. Then again, he had the means to have a copy of the portrait made. I shoved the thought out of my head. That was preposterous.

"We haven't discovered who," Alfred added. "But when we do, we'll find Mother's portrait."

Anna turned to Alfred. "Thank you," she said. "Thank you for trying to clear my son's name."

120

"It was all Katherine," Alfred said. "She insisted we keep investigating, just in case Samuel was innocent, like he insisted."

"She wouldn't give up," Maxwell added, a hint of pride in his voice.

"But I had lots of help from my sister, Maxwell, and Alfred. And we still won't give up," I told Anna. "We'll keep at it until we find out who tried to frame you."

"I'm very impressed by this new generation of courageous young women," Anna said. "You'll do well in the world. Of that I'm sure."

"Does this mean the wedding is back on?" Alfred asked, his eyes on his father. Then he turned to Anna. "Please say it is."

Henry Vandermeer's eyes flitted from Anna to Alfred and back again. He took Anna's hands. She didn't resist him. I felt a flicker of hope in my heart.

"Please forgive me," Henry said to Anna. "I should have believed you from the very beginning. It was all just too much, and I'm sorry I let myself get carried away." He shook his head. "I'll never doubt you again, my love. If you can forgive me this foolishness, my greatest wish in the world would be to marry you. Tomorrow, as planned."

Anna wiped away tears—tears of happiness this time. "Henry, I don't want to live without you. I do want to be your wife, forever and always."

Henry nodded gravely, too overcome to speak.

"You can ask me anything, anytime, and I promise that I'll always tell you the truth," she said, her voice thick with tears. "But you must promise me that you mean it when you say you won't doubt me, or my son, again. I must know that as my husband you'll trust in me, as I will trust in you."

Elizabeth and I were soon wiping away happy tears of our own. Even Uncle Willem's stormy eyes were misting over.

"Can I tell everyone the wedding is back on?" Alfred asked eagerly.

"Yes!" Anna and Henry said, not taking their eyes off each other. "The wedding is on!"

Before I knew it, the servants were hustling and bustling about, putting in place all of the wedding preparations they had begun to dismantle. Elizabeth and I were rushed away to our fittings with the dressmaker from New York City who had sewn our beautiful bridesmaids' gowns. Everyone seemed happy and satisfied that the wedding was going to take place after all.

But I couldn't be completely satisfied. I was pleased beyond measure that Anna and Henry would be married after all, but the original portrait was still missing. There were three more important questions still outstanding: Who had tried to frame Anna and Samuel? Would he or she try to stop the wedding again? And where was the first Mrs. Vandermeer's portrait? Louisa Branson and her fictional Miss Millhouse wouldn't have given up until they answered these questions, and neither would I.

At dinner that night, I kept my eyes on all the guests and on the servants, too. Everywhere I looked, however, I saw nothing but delight. I watched Uncle Willem, remembering Samuel's belief that he wasn't happy about the wedding, but he toasted the couple and laughed with Papa and was the good-humored man I had come to know and admire.

Samuel, who seemed relieved and even a little

happy himself, noticed the direction of my gaze. "I won't fully believe that wedding is going to take place until I stand up beside Henry tomorrow," he said. "But I am hopeful that whoever tried to stop the wedding has given up."

"Stand up beside Henry?" Maxwell asked. "Are you to be his best man? Not Alfred?"

That surprised me, too. I would have expected Alfred to stand with his father.

Samuel shook his head. "Henry thought it would be a symbol of our new, united family if I was his best man. Alfred agreed. He's content to join Maxwell in walking you and your sister down the aisle."

I glanced over at Alfred, deep in conversation with my sister, Elizabeth, about a sailing trip he and his father had taken to the West Indies.

Samuel smiled. "If he could stop talking to Elizabeth about his adventures on the high seas long enough, Alfred could tell you so himself."

The two of them looked up upon hearing their names. Elizabeth's cheeks were flushed at the idea of adventure.

"Tell you what?" Alfred asked.

He confirmed what Samuel had told us, and then he and Elizabeth went back to their discussion concerning what he had discovered about island life.

"Who will walk your mother down the aisle?" I asked.

Samuel frowned. "Uncle Willem, I suppose," he said.

"Don't worry. There's no stopping this wedding now," I assured him. "Tomorrow will be the best of days."

"I hope you're right," Samuel answered.

The next morning dawned bright and sunny. I woke before Essie entered the room, excited about the day ahead.

My beautiful bridesmaid dress hung on a hook on the outside of the closet, where nothing would cause it to wrinkle. I had no doubt that Elizabeth and I would be the best-dressed ladies at the wedding, with the exception of the bride, of course. The only thing that would have made our ensembles more perfect was if we could wear our pendants with them. We had tried the day before, during our fittings, but we reluctantly agreed that they covered too much of the lovely embroidery on the bodice. We would have to be content with wearing our mother's gift on the inside of our dresses. Neither one of us could imagine going without them completely.

Essie brought us our breakfast on a tray. The household staff was busy getting the dining room ready for the wedding lunch.

"Nothing happened overnight to put a stop to the wedding, did it?" I asked as soon as she entered the room.

"Not a thing. Don't you worry," she said. "I just passed Tabitha in the hall with Mrs. DuMay's breakfast tray. She was whistling a happy tune and smiling from ear to ear."

"I am relieved," I said.

Elizabeth and I both slipped on easy day dresses so that we could breakfast on the balcony. The servants had set up a white tent on the manor's vast green lawn overlooking the ocean and were now setting up rows of chairs with an aisle in between. They unrolled a white carpet in the aisle and then came the flowers! It was all absolutely beautiful. I decided then and there that my own wedding would be outdoors, too, in the gardens of Chatswood Manor.

Essie bustled about our rooms, making our beds and examining our dresses for any hint of a wrinkle or a loose thread. We had barely finished breakfast and bathed before it was time to dress.

Elizabeth dressed first. I followed her and Essie into her bedchamber. Before Essie even had a chance to fasten the tiny seed pearl buttons that ran up the back of the dress, Elizabeth began to twirl to show off her flounced skirt.

"Wouldn't it be wonderful if the original portrait turned up before the wedding?" she mused. "Alfred will be heartbroken if it's not returned. He's such a fine young man; I would hate to see him unhappy."

"I'm sure that's Anna's wish as well," I said. "Who do you think might have tried to frame her and Samuel?"

"I can't imagine. Everyone we've encountered seems delighted with the match." She stopped twirling long enough for Essie to begin on her buttons. There must have been a hundred.

"Even Samuel," I said, "despite his misgivings about Uncle Willem. He does want his mother to be happy."

"I do think he's mistaken about Uncle Willem," Elizabeth said. "He has been nothing but friendly with

127

Anna, as far as I can tell, and he made such a lovely toast last night."

"He may have some insight into who took the portrait, though," I said. "Maybe if I share my notes with him, he'll be able to shed some light onto what might have happened to the original. And he's the one who designed and built Vandermeer Manor. He would know more than anyone else about these hidden passageways."

Elizabeth stood back so that we could admire her in the dress.

"You are a beauty, Lady Elizabeth," Essie said. "But your hair isn't! How is it that you manage to get it so tangled in your sleep? If I didn't know better, I'd think elves came in the night to make more work for me," she teased.

Elizabeth sat at her dressing table, looked in the mirror, and giggled. Her hair was indeed a sight. "Now that we know you're Irish, Essie, I'd say it was leprechauns."

"I wish we could blame the missing portrait on leprechauns," I said with a smile. "While you're doing my sister's hair, Essie, I'm going to look for

Uncle Willem. It would be nice to have this matter settled before the wedding."

I ran downstairs and checked the parlor first in the hopes that the portrait had been returned, but it had not. Uncle Willem wasn't there. Nor was he in the library, but one of the footmen said he had just gone to his quarters to get ready for the wedding.

Back upstairs, I entered the wing with the family's rooms. I found Uncle Willem's door ajar. He was giving instructions to someone, no doubt his valet, about his white tailcoat. I was about to knock when the voice of the man who answered him sent shivers down my spine.

It was the same deep voice I had heard in the night—the one in the secret passage that spoke of a portrait.

Uncle Willem's valet had something to do with the theft of the painting!

$\mathscr{I}$ backed away from the door and the voice. Why would Uncle Willem's valet have been sneaking around in the middle of the night, talking about portraits? And who was his accomplice?

I knew I must tell Uncle Willem right away, even with that horrid man in the room. I was trying to find the courage when Essie found me.

"It's time to dress, milady, or you'll be late for the wedding," she said.

"But I have to talk to—"

"Whatever it is, it can wait," she said. "You don't want to hold up the wedding ceremony, not after all that's happened."

"But—"

At that moment, either Uncle Willem or his valet noticed the door was ajar and closed it firmly. My news would have to wait until after the ceremony. I just hoped the valet didn't have any other tricks planned to stop the wedding.

Alone in my room with Elizabeth and Essie, I told them what I had discovered.

"Have you gotten to know Uncle Willem's valet at all, Essie?" I asked. "Do you have any idea why he would do such a terrible thing?"

Essie shook her head. "He seems like a good worker, but I haven't seen much of him. I assume that Mr. Vandermeer must demand a lot of attention. The valet—Abbot, I think his name is—is quite friendly with the head housemaid. I see them whispering a lot. And yesterday they had a definite quarrel."

"Do you know anything about her?" I asked.

"She arrived at Vandermeer Manor on the day Willem Vandermeer moved in," Essie said. "She's quite proud about that and tells anyone with ears to hear her. Started as a scullery maid and is now the head housemaid."

I felt more confused than ever. Why would a valet and a housemaid try to stop the wedding? The only thing left to do was speak to Uncle Willem.

Papa knocked on our door then and told us it was time to join the wedding party. I took his arm. "Elizabeth, you're absolutely stunning," he said.

My sister, Elizabeth, took his other arm. "And you, Katherine."

Elizabeth's eyes danced with amusement. I agreed with a slight nod not to point out our dear papa's mistake.

"Thank you, Papa," I said. "I've missed you. You've been so busy with Uncle Willem and Cousin Henry that we've hardly seen you."

"I've missed you, too, my dear. Weddings remind me that my time with the two of you is precious," he said to my sister and me. "As soon as the festivities are over and things calm down, the three of us are going to have a long talk."

"And a walk on the beach?" my sister asked.

Papa laughed. "Yes, Katherine. I see you've changed your mind about the ocean. We'll go for a long walk on the beach and see if we can spy any dolphins."

We entered the parlor to join the wedding party. I hated to see the blank space on the wall where Mrs. Vandermeer's portrait had hung, but Alfred seemed calm and happy. He and Maxwell stood together, chatting.

We rushed up to them, giggling about Papa's mistake.

"Why don't we continue the charade?" Maxwell said with a grin. "Alfred can walk down the aisle with Lady Elizabeth. And I'll walk with Katherine."

"That's a splendid idea," Elizabeth said, clapping her hands. "We'll fool everyone here."

I looked away so that Maxwell would not see my blush. He followed my gaze to the blank space on the wall.

"I know you must be disappointed," he said. "I'm sure the Vandermeers can find someone to make a copy of the copy—one that isn't damaged. Alfred will have that, at least."

"But I have discovered something more—" I began.

I was about to share my latest news when Anna walked into the room on Samuel's arm. The bride was truly beautiful, glowing with happiness and wearing a dress that belonged in one of my fairy stories.

Henry Vandermeer couldn't take his eyes off her.

"My darling," Anna said, looking into his eyes. "I

am so happy." Then she turned to Uncle William and raised her hand, as if to take his arm.

Uncle Willem stepped back and shook his head. "I'm sorry, my dear. I cannot walk you down the aisle."

Samuel stepped forward, his hands balled into fists.

"Whatever do you mean, Uncle?" Henry Vandermeer asked.

"I am not worthy of such an honor," Uncle Willem answered. "I am deeply ashamed to tell you that I am responsible for all that has happened the past few days. I was the one who wished to stop the wedding."

Nearly everyone in the room gasped—everyone except Samuel. His eyes flashed with anger. "I knew it," he said.

Henry was genuinely perplexed. "But you weren't even here the day the portrait disappeared," Henry said.

"I don't understand, Uncle Willem," Alfred added.

Uncle Willem explained that he had had a copy of the portrait made. His valet had stayed behind at Vandermeer Manor instead of traveling to Providence. He knew all of the manor's secret passageways, and along with the help of the head housemaid, had removed the original and placed the defaced copy in

Anna's closet. In fact, the housemaid had stolen some paints from one of the other servants to deface the copy herself.

"I made sure you thought my valet was in Providence with me, but in fact he simply kept to my quarters and the secret passageways while I was away. He was able to slip in and out of the parlor while the rest of the house was occupied. It was the work of a moment.

"I was going to put the original portrait back in its place after all the excitement had died down and I was sure the wedding wouldn't take place," he continued.

Anna was pale and trembling. "Why would your staff do such a thing to me? To Henry and Alfred?" she asked.

"They're loyal to me, and I paid them well for their efforts," Uncle Willem admitted. "I do apologize, Henry. It was a terrible thing to do." He turned to Anna and Samuel. "I owe you an even deeper apology."

"I still don't understand," Anna said. "Why would you try to destroy our happiness?"

"I thought you were marrying Henry for his money. Why would an independent woman, one who wants to have a career as a writer, marry for any other reason? Money and position in society—that's what I thought you wanted."

"But Henry and I love and respect each other," Anna said quietly. "That is our reason for marrying. I would never marry for money."

"I see that now. I saw it when you forgave Henry so readily and so lovingly yesterday afternoon. I saw it when you lit up with happiness to know that the wedding would take place after all. I hope you can forgive the prejudice of an old man who is a bit perplexed by this modern world."

Henry and Anna exchanged a quiet look.

"Of course I can, Uncle," Anna said, kissing him on the cheek. "As long as you can assure me that the portrait of the first Mrs. Vandermeer will hang in the parlor long after Alfred is married and grown old himself."

"I'll have it taken care of immediately," Uncle Willem said.

He excused himself to see to it, but we were still left with the question of who would walk Anna down the aisle. Papa was suggested and Samuel. But Anna had another idea.

"Why don't we walk each other down the aisle?" she suggested to Henry.

He agreed that it was a splendid notion.

The bridesmaids and groomsmen lined up.

Cousin Maxwell, with a twinkle in his eye, held out his arm to me.

I heard Papa comment as we passed by. He had slipped into the last row of seats, next to Essie, just as the processional music began. "Lady Elizabeth and Lord Maxwell make a handsome couple, do they not?"

Essie's eyes danced. She could tell us apart even when Papa couldn't. "Yes, milord," she said. "They do."

I stood across from Maxwell, listening to Anna and Henry pledge to love and honor each other forever. He stared into my eyes for a moment and then looked away, his cheeks red.

As we filed out after the now married couple, he whispered in my ear, "The bride left the word 'obey' out of her wedding vows, Katherine," he said. "Did you notice?"

"I did," I whispered back. "She replaced it with the word 'cherish.' Much nicer, don't you agree?"

The wedding reception was fit for royalty, with a

lavish meal, a full orchestra, and lots and lots of dancing.

Cousin Maxwell and I took a break from the dancing to walk through the gardens. We had a long talk about Miss Millhouse—I had given him two of Louisa Branson's published stories to read the night before—and about the scary Mr. Poe. I promised to give his stories a try.

We had just joined the party again when I noticed that even the ocean seemed to celebrate the marriage. The waves were gentle and didn't overpower the orchestra with a fierce roar. Midway through the afternoon, a school of dolphins saluted the couple by leaping and dancing to the music.

After the wedding cake was served and the guests began to leave, Elizabeth and I sat on a small garden bench to catch our breath while Maxwell and Alfred went to get us some punch.

Elizabeth's eyes followed Alfred as he stopped to greet one of his father's guests and then caught up with Maxwell again.

"I'm going to miss America when we go back home," she said quietly.

"That's weeks and weeks away," I said.

"Yes, but still . . ." Her voice trailed off.

I watched Maxwell make his way back toward me, his eyes bright. When we returned to England, I wouldn't see him every day as I did now.

"I'll miss it, too," I said. "I love Chatswood Manor, but America is splendid. I'm glad we'll be here for a few weeks more. Let's just hope we don't stumble across any more mysteries to solve," I said.

Elizabeth laughed. "Or maybe we should hope that we do."

Every
Secrets of the Manor
book leads to another.

Read on for a first look at
Betsy's Story,
1934

"*Voilà!*" Madame Lorraine exclaimed as she stepped away from the dais. "You may open your eyes, Lady Betsy."

My breath caught in my chest. For weeks, Madame Lorraine, the famous Parisian dressmaker, had been working on a custom gown for my twelfth birthday ball—which was less than a month away! And now the gown was nearly ready; all that was left for Madame Lorraine to do was add the trim. I kept my eyes shut for another second to savor the anticipation.

Then I looked in the mirror.

Was that really me looking back?

My new ball gown was the most gorgeous dress I'd ever seen. It was the color of the sky on a summery day; Madame Lorraine had ordered the shimmery silk charmeuse fabric all the way from China. The gown had capped sleeves and a fluttery skirt that hit just below my knees. Madame Lorraine's creation was more gorgeous than I'd imagined it could be. And it wasn't even finished yet!

I shivered—just the tiniest bit, really—but Mum noticed, of course, like she always noticed everything.

"Have you taken a chill, Betsy?" she asked, nodding at the goose prickles on my bare arms.

"A little," I replied. "But mostly I'm excited!"

A knowing smile crossed Mum's face. "Of course you are," she said. Then she nodded at my new lady's maid, Maggie. "But perhaps it is a bit too drafty in here for a fitting."

Mum didn't need to say another word; Maggie immediately crossed the room to close the windows. The April sunshine was so bright and cheery that we'd all wanted to enjoy it through the open windows without giving much thought to the chill in the morning air.

"It's coming along beautifully, Madame Lorraine," Mum continued. "What a lovely silhouette! So very modern."

"*Merci*, Lady Beth," said Madame Lorraine. "Have

you and Lady Betsy selected the embellishments?"

"Yes, we have," Mum replied. "We adore the velvet ribbon, but the satin ribbon will be more appropriate for the season. And while the purple beads have a lovely sheen, they don't hold a candle to the gold ones. Nellie, would you please fetch them?"

"Certainly, milady," Nellie, Mum's lady's maid, replied. Madame Lorraine had brought an entire trunk of trim with her—rolls of ribbons in every color, sparkling beads and rhinestones, and silk flowers more delicate than anything in the garden. It had been almost impossible to choose! In the end, though, Mum and I had both agreed that the shiny satin ribbon and sparkly gold beads would be just the thing to complement the gown—and the Elizabeth necklace, a precious family heirloom that I would receive on the day I turned twelve.

Every firstborn daughter in my family had been named Elizabeth in honor of my great-great-grandmother Elizabeth, who had been born almost one hundred years ago. We took different variations on the name "Elizabeth" for our nicknames—I went by Betsy, for example, while my mum went by Beth—but we were all Elizabeths, just like her. But there was even more to the family legacy than our names. There was the Elizabeth necklace.

When Great-Great-Grandmother Elizabeth turned twelve, she received a stunning gold pendant in the shape of half a heart, which was set with brilliant blue sapphires. Elizabeth's twin sister, Katherine, had received a nearly identical necklace, but it was set with fiery red rubies instead. The necklaces weren't just beautiful; they were deeply significant to each twin, since they were carefully chosen by their beloved mother, who died just a few months before their birthday. Their mother didn't live to celebrate their birthdays with them, so the special gift she left for each of them became their most cherished possession.

When the two pendants were put together, they formed a single, whole heart, which was a perfect symbol for Elizabeth and Katherine, as they were almost never apart. But after the girls grew up, family obligations forced them to separate. As the slightly older twin, Elizabeth had been pledged to marry her cousin, Maxwell Chatswood, in order to keep Chatswood Manor in the family. Meanwhile, Katherine had fallen in love with Alfred Vandermeer, and shortly after marrying, they emigrated from England to America, where her new husband founded Vandermeer Steel. The family lived in the beautiful and stately Vandermeer Manor, overlooking the ocean in Rhode Island. That's where my cousin Kay Vandermeer Wilson, Katherine's great-great-granddaughter, lived today. Kay and I weren't just cousins; we were best friends, even though we'd never met. We had so much in common—we both loved *Hollywood Hello* magazine (me for the articles about radio plays, Kay for the photos of movie stars), dogs were our favorite animals, and our birthdays were just a month apart. And in two weeks, Kay and I would finally meet when she and her parents—Aunt Kate and Uncle Joseph—arrived in England to help celebrate my birthday! I already knew that meeting Cousin Kay for the first time would be the very best birthday present of all.

And to make things even more exciting, Mum and Aunt Kate had promised to tell Kay and me a secret on my birthday. A *big* secret that had been in the Chatswood family for generations. For months now, Kay and I had been trying to find out what it was. But neither Mum nor Aunt Kate would say another word about it. The suspense was driving us mad!

I shifted my weight ever so slightly as Mum and Madame Lorraine discussed the trim we'd selected.

"I think some beads around the neck, *oui*, and perhaps the sleeves," Madame Lorraine said through a mouthful of pins. "Not too much, of course. Nothing ostentatious. A beauty like Lady Betsy needs no adornment; she will shine all on her own!"

I flushed with pleasure at the compliment. It was an honor to have Madame Lorraine design my ball gown. My mother's French cousin, Gabrielle, had surprised us by insisting that Madame Lorraine, her personal dressmaker, travel all the way to Chatswood Manor just to make my special birthday dress. In a few weeks, Cousin Gabrielle would also be joining us for the birthday festivities. I scarcely knew Gabby, whose glamorous life in Paris kept her too busy for country holidays at Chatswood Manor, but I was excited about having a house full of visitors. Ever since my father died when I was just a baby, Mum and I had been on our own. We made a good team—Mum and I did almost everything together—but sometimes I secretly wished that our little family were larger. What a change it would be to have the Wilsons and Cousin Gabby at Chatswood Manor! Just the thought of laughter at breakfast and cozy evenings in the parlor made me smile. I knew Mum was as eager as I was for our extended family to arrive.

"You know, I am having another thought," Madame Lorraine mused. She snipped a length of ribbon off the roll, her silver scissors flashing in the sunlight. "What if we add a belt from this ribbon, like so? I will make a buckle to match . . . perhaps even embroider some beads on it. . . ."

"A belt? Instead of a sash?" Mum said, frowning a little. "Wouldn't that be a bit casual?"

"*Non, non.* I can assure you, it is the very latest fashion in Paris," replied Madame Lorraine.

"What do you think, Betsy?" Mum asked me.

"Yes! I love that idea," I said. "I think a beaded belt would be smashing."

"How much times have changed since my own birthday ball," Mum said. "My gown was blue as well, but entirely different in style. It was full length, with a gorgeous overskirt made of shimmery tulle. And I wore gloves with my gown, of course—gloves that stretched all the way past my elbows."

"Ahh, *oui,* gloves for Lady Betsy as well, I think," Madame Lorraine said.

"Well, I'm glad to know that fashions haven't changed *that* much," Mum said with a laugh.

"I remember when Miss Kate—I suppose I should call her Mrs. Wilson—was getting ready for her twelfth birthday ball," Nellie reminisced. "She *hated* her fittings—called them frightfully dull wastes of time. The dressmaker was forever begging her to stand still!"

We all laughed—even Madame Lorraine.

"Then one day, I started reading to Miss Kate to take her mind off the torture of her fittings," Nellie continued. "It did the trick. We had a bit of a reading club back then. Oh, we loved stories more than anyone else in Vandermeer Manor."

"But not more than me," I teased. "Tell me the story, Nellie, of how you came to England. Please!" I always wanted to hear about how Mum's maid, Shannon, had fallen in love with the Vandermeers' chauffeur, Hank, when Mum had visited Aunt Kate as a girl. Rather than watch Shannon return to England and leave true love behind, Mum and Aunt Kate had conspired to help Nellie and Shannon switch places! It was a thrilling and romantic tale, the sort of story I would expect to hear on the radio during one of my favorite programs. I could hardly believe it had happened in real life!

"A favorite story, to be sure," Mum said, "but I think some refreshments are in order first. Would you mind fetching a tray from the kitchen?"

"I'll go," Maggie volunteered.

"No, no. You stay in case Lady Betsy needs anything," Nellie said. "I'll be back in a jiffy."

"There," Madame Lorraine announced. "What do you think of the belt? I will add the beads later, of course."

"Oh, it's perfect!" I cried.

"Very cunning," Mum said, sounding pleased. "The perfect accoutrement!"

There was a soft rap at the door. It was one of the footmen, Adam.

"Beg your pardon, milady," he said to Mum, "but you've a telephone call. Long-distance, from America."

"America!" I cried. "It's got to be Aunt Kate!"

*I*n one swift motion, Mum rose to her feet. "If you'll excuse me, Madame Lorraine," she said smoothly. "But I must take this call."

"Mum! Wait for me!" I spoke up.

But she had already hurried out of the room.

I jumped off the dais and felt a dozen pins stab me where Madame Lorraine had placed the ribbon. "Ow!" I cried.

"Wait, please, *mademoiselle*," Madame Lorraine urged. "Do not move until I loosen the pins."

"Maggie, would you help her, please?" I said. It was a rare treat to talk to our American relatives on the phone, and I didn't want to miss a moment of it. Mum always let me sit beside her and listen to her part of the conversation. And best of all, sometimes Mum even let me say hello to Cousin Kay!

The minutes ticked away while Maggie and Madame Lorraine loosened the pins enough for me to wriggle out of the gown.

"Would you like to wear your pink dress again, Lady Betsy?" Maggie asked, moving slower than a swan as she reached for the dress I'd chosen that morning. "Or did you have another ensemble in mind for the afternoon?"

I took one look at the dainty buttons on the dress and shook my head. "There's no time for that," I replied as I reached for my silk dressing gown. I flung the gown over my starched white slip and bolted from the room, tying the sash as I hurried down the stairs toward the library. There I found Mum, holding on to the edge of her oak desk as if to steady herself.

"Oh, Kate," she said into the receiver. "Oh, no . . ."

The expression on Mum's face—a strangled look of shock and dismay—was not one I would soon forget. I just knew that the news was bad. *Oh, please,* I thought. *Not Kay. Not Uncle Joseph. Please let them be all right.*

Without saying a word, I reached for Mum's hand. She was so engrossed in the call that I don't think she noticed me until she felt the warmth of my touch.

Mum pulled her hand from my grasp and covered the mouthpiece.

"Betsy, I need to speak privately with Aunt Kate."

"But I—"

"Not now," she said firmly.

Then Mum returned to the telephone, keeping her eyes fixed on me as I left the library. She didn't start speaking again until I reached the door.

I stood alone in the hallway, stunned, trying to understand what had just happened. Mum had never asked me to leave the library while she was on the telephone—*never*. And especially not when she was talking to Aunt Kate! Something terrible must have happened, and the longer I stood there, the heavier my worries grew. How could I possibly wait until Mum was off the phone to find out what had happened?

Suddenly, I realized that my hand was still on the doorknob. And the door was still open a crack. In my shock, I had neglected to close it all the way.

If I leaned forward—if I didn't make a single sound—it was entirely possible that I could still hear Mum's part of the conversation.

It wouldn't be wrong to listen in, I tried to convince

myself. *Mum and I don't have secrets from each other. Not even one. And I'm sure she'll tell me everything later, anyway. She always does.*

Holding my breath, I leaned toward the sliver of light peeking through the crack. Sure enough, I could hear Mum's voice if I strained my ears. I concentrated all my energy on listening, doing my best to ignore the guilt prickling at my conscience.

"But, Kate, I don't know why he would—surely he *knew*—of course, of course—"

"Lady Betsy!"

I spun around as if I'd been caught with my hand in the cookie jar. Maggie had crept up behind me so quietly that I hadn't even noticed her—not until her words pierced my ears. *Oh, no—what if Mum heard her, too?* I wondered.

sew zoey

If you love the gorgeous gowns
in Secrets of the Manor,
wait until you meet Zoey Webber,
a seventh-grade fashion designer!
Check out the Sew Zoey books,
available at your favorite store!